DANGEROUS GAMES

CORRUPT BLOODLINES
BOOK ONE

LYDIA HALL

ALSO BY LYDIA HALL

Series: Spicy Office Secrets

New Beginnings || Corporate Connection || Caught in the Middle ||
Faking It For The Boss || Baby Makes Three || The Boss's Secret || My
Best Friend's Dad

Series: The Big Bad Braddock Brothers

Burning Love || Tell Me You Love Me || Second Chance at Love ||
Pregnant: Who is the Father? || Pregnant with the Bad Boy

Series: The Forbidden Attraction

My Mommy's Boyfriend || Daddy's Best Friend || Daddy Undercover ||
The Doctor's Twins || She's Mine

BLURB

Rich, powerful, cruel, older and dominant. I'm everything she hates... and everything she can't resist.

Nanette Slater is my new hitman's sister. Unfortunately for the pretty brunette, her brother is no good at his job, which means Nanette ends up kidnapped and in my bed...

Unless he makes good on his promise, I'm keeping his sister to myself. Not that I'm complaining.

She's pretty irresistible despite the age gap, and the longer she spends in my home, the harder it is to resist her forbidden curves. I'm a man after all... A man her brother despises. But I'm not going to let that stop me.

Nanette's brother may think I'm a good for nothing criminal, but she makes her own decisions. And as soon as my dominant nature comes out, poor, pretty little Nanette is going to fall for me.

Hard.

DANGEROUS GAMES is the first book of The Corrupt Bloodlines series. This dark, sensual, twisted romance novel does *not* hold back on the spice!

DOMINIC

I sit in my car watching the house. He's in there with his sister, a union I won't disrupt for now, so long as he does what I tell him to do. But I won't wait long. Men like Jimmy Slater have a lot of skills but not a lot of loyalty, and if he tries to turn tail and run, I'll be in hot water, so I'm forced to sit on his tiny little craftsman home and wait until he's unoccupied. I've done this a few times; each time his sister is here, and God knows what she is trying to tell him or what he's told her.

The door opens, and the leggy brunette walks out. Her curly hair hangs around her thin, curvy frame. It's abnormal. She usually has it tied up, but today I get to enjoy her in all her splendor. She stands on the top step looking up at her brother and I admire that ass of hers, perky and tight, like she runs or something. It doesn't hurt that she is wearing heels and a pair of jeans that are so tight they look like they were painted on.

My cock twitches just looking at her. She is delectable, and I am a hungry man. I'd take a bite of that any time, but right now I can't be distracted. Not with the issues I'm facing. And Jimmy better come through for me, or maybe I'll end up finding a way to have my just desserts and a little icing on the cake. Nanette Slater could be just the icing I'm looking for.

She turns, stepping down the stairs, and looks right at my car. I know she can't see me; the windows are tinted too dark. But she has a scowl on her face. I wonder if Jimmy told her what he was up to, but he is smart. I've threatened him enough that he should know better. My business is private, and I don't usually have to tell people twice. What I've hired him to do is even more dangerous than a normal hit, and I've selected the best hitman in the city who isn't part of the family.

When Nanette is more than a block away, I step out of my car and button my coat. The piece conveniently holstered on my right hip is discreet. No one would know it's there if I don't tell them. But Jimmy will know. He knows who I am, and what I'm capable of.

The neighborhood is quiet, the sound of a lawnmower in the distance and some birds chirping is all I can hear. Jimmy won't be expecting me, though he should have something to report at least. The job shouldn't be taking this long. I gave him access to all my resources— the loyal ones anyway. And he has unlimited funds, courtesy of my credit card. There is no reason for him to be dawdling like this.

I jam my finger into the doorbell button and hear the chime on the other side of the door. Then I fold my hands in front of myself casually and wait. The smell of cat urine wafts up to my nose and I am disgusted. At least he could hose off his porch if he isn't going to chase the strays away. Jimmy has some poor hygiene habits when it comes to animals.

The door swings open and his face is buried in his phone. "What, Nan? You forget something?" His eyes sweep up to meet my gaze and they go wide. "Oh... Dom, hey, buddy. I'm, uh... I have."

"Move," I tell him, stepping across the threshold. He backs into his home frightened—as he well should be. He's taking too long, and he knows it. "Shut the door." I walk into his living room and stand directly beneath the light mounted in the center of the ceiling. The old area rug dampens my footsteps across the wood planks, but Jimmy's stockinged feet make no noise as he moves. A trained killer makes no noise when he moves; that's how I knew Jimmy was good at the first interview.

"Uh, Dom, I just. I'm sorry. I got delayed and—"

"Shut up." I look around the room. Everything is as it was the last time I came. He is less than a neat freak, but not a slob—except for the stray cats on the porch. The old home has seen better days though, a problem Jimmy could remedy if he just finished this job. He has a payout coming that's bigger than he's ever dreamed. "Tell me what you have."

His sniveling behavior is repugnant. He talks in circles, spouting things he told me last time. "The money all ties back to an offshore account. The payouts are going to someone named Henry Watts. He's a man of means, ex-military. I'm not sure—"

"Cut the crap, Jimmy." My voice startles him, and he jumps. By now he's got to have uncovered the truth about my identity. I never tried to hide it; I just didn't announce it before he accepted the job because men like him don't tend to get in bed with my type. At least not on their own accord.

"Dom, please, you have to understand that if I knew you were Bratva I'd have turned this job down. I'm not capable of this." He shoves his phone in his pocket and shakes his head, and it stirs my temper. He does not want to stir my temper.

"What did you say, Jimmy? I think you said you weren't going to do what you told me you'd do. Now if I remember correctly, I gave you some pretty nice compensation already. Access to every bit of intel I have. Unlimited funds. The power to even hurt me. And now you're backing out?" I take a step toward him, and he cowers, holding his hands up in a defensive posture.

"Dom, please. It doesn't have to go down this way, okay? I swear I won't tell a soul." He shakes his head as he backs into the wall and I advance on him slowly, a monster hunting his prey.

"You know that's not how this works, Jimmy. You are a smart man. You should have figured this out already." I unbutton my coat and pull out my Smith and Wesson and Jimmy literally whimpers. What a fucking coward. He calls himself a hitman? "Now, you are supposed to produce results for me. I need to know who hired the hit, and who is doing the hit. You have three days to figure this out, or you're not going to like me at all."

"Dom, woah," he says, his voice quavering. "Look, buddy, I'm not that good. At best I need two weeks, but this is tricky shit. I can't just tell you anything; I have to have the truth. That's what you want, right? Facts?"

I chamber a round and lean in so I know he hears me when I say, "Three days, Slater."

"That's insane. I can't do the—"

The gun goes off right next to his ear, firing a round through the wall and launching it into the wall on the other side of the adjoining kitchen. No doubt he'll find a hole in his siding out the back of the house. He winces, covering his ear and shouting. "Three days, Jimmy, or maybe we have a talk about writing your will."

"Fuck, what'd you do that for?"

"Consider it a friendly reminder that you are mine. You're on my payroll, which makes you just as guilty as me. You want to back out; well, I clean up all my mess. I don't leave loose ends hanging."

"God, Dominic, you have to understand I have a family too. I can't get wrapped up in this mess. I want a good life." He's busy rubbing his ringing ear when I bring the butt of my gun down hard on his shoulder, and he drops to his knees.

"Your family will appreciate that you are a hard-working man the instant you finish this job and give me what I want. You should have done your homework before accepting the job. Now you have three days to finish it, or—"

"I know, I know!" he shouts, which is the wrong move. My foot connects to his gut and he curls into a ball.

With my message sent, I slip out the front door as if nothing happened, and stroll to my car. At least it's a pleasant day. The sun is shining, and I have other business to tend to. So, when I climb into my car I head straight back to the office—my little slice of heaven in the back of the bookstore. I can't help but let my eyes linger on Nanette's ass as I pass her, now several blocks away and still walking. It sparks an idea in my mind of absconding with her and having my way in the back of my car, but business comes first.

I pull up to the bookstore and park in my usual spot. The boys are waiting for me; I'm certain of it. I was due in an hour ago, but Nanette took such a long time doing whatever it was with Jimmy that I had no choice. The instant I walk in I'm bombarded by questions. These guys are worse than a pack of yapping chihuahuas.

"Look, we've been waiting for an hour. What the hell happened?"

"Yeah, boss, there's a shipment coming, and we need your signature on the paperwork or—"

"Shut up," I snap, leading them into my office. I click on the lights and sit behind my desk. No one rushes me, and no one tells me how to do my job. Besides the fact that I can't tell them a single thing about Jimmy Slater or his task for me. This is an inside job; I know that much is true, and I don't have the means to sniff it out entirely by myself. Only, I don't know who to trust, who is loyal. "Sit down."

Nick and Leo sit across from me, both of them with resting bitch face, but I don't care. I'm in charge here and they do as I say. Nick crosses one leg over the other and leans back like he owns the joint, and Leo shakes his head, haughty and about to be taken down a notch. I unholster my gun, tucked there safely after I nearly made Jimmy deaf, and lay it on the desk. That sobers them and they look less hostile.

"The guns, they're due in tomorrow. Who is on that shipment?"

"We heard it's going to be the same guy as last time." Nick's report doesn't please me, but I'm not surprised. The Armenian arms dealer we work with has gotten sloppy and can't be trusted much longer.

"Put three extra men on it then. We can't afford a slip up. And Leo, I want you on the roof. Put the rifle on the truck. If something goes down, blow the tires first. If he doesn't stop, aim for his forehead." Leo nods, they understand my instructions and I know they will follow through, even if they are part of the problem here. "Now, where is the paperwork?"

Nick reaches into his jacket pocket and pulls out a folded bundle of papers. I take them and unfold them to see the order for seventy AR rifles is in order. I scrawl my name across the bottom and push the papers back to him, and he puts them back into his pocket. This crap is getting old, and I'm ready to move up, let my brother Sven take this over so I can do the real work of running this family, but only once I've proven my worth to my father.

"Get out," I tell them, ready to stew on my anger over Jimmy. They scurry away like scared little mice, and I sit back in my chair and listen to the door click shut. Someone in my organization has hired a man to kill me. I'm not sure if it is Nick or Leo. For all I know it could be one of my brothers too. They each have motive—to unseat me as the next Pakhan so they can take my rightful throne, though I don't truly suspect any of the four of them.

I pinch the bridge of my nose, breathing out a deep sigh. This stress isn't nearly as bad as some of the situations I've been in before, but it's right up there, and the only thing that takes the edge off is a good fuck. Too bad Nanette Slater is a little out of my reach at the moment, but if Jimmy doesn't play his cards right, I may just have to leverage her. She'd look really good bent over the end of my desk or spread wide on my bed. And just thinking of that makes my dick go hard.

I pull out my phone and flip through the pictures I took while I was waiting for Jimmy the last few times I showed up at his house. Nanette is in every single one of them, though some catch my eye more than others. Like this one where she's wearing a tight miniskirt. She dropped something and had to bend to pick it up, and as she did, I got a glimpse of the black panties she wore.

While Nanette is definitely worth feasting my eyes on, she's more valuable than that. Jimmy has a soft spot for her. I've seen it with my own eyes. She snapped at him about not feeding the strays and the very same day he removed the food dish from the front porch. Maybe I could use that weakness against him, force him to cooperate with me and maybe enjoy something I want on the side too.

Right now, Jimmy is a liability. He knows too much about me and my organization. If he were to rat, I'd go down, plain and simple. I need some insurance that he's going to do what I say, and Nanette might just be what I need. The minute he pulls that trigger, he will be just as guilty as me though, and that's what I'm counting on. Once he's done, he's done. He would go down as hard as I did if he ratted. And maybe Nanette could be just the thing to force him to finish what he started.

One thing is certain, I have to root out the mole and protect myself or there will be no organization left. At least not how it is today. My life depends on it, and so does my position in this family and I know Jimmy Slater is the only man who can do this. With my help of course. And maybe a little nudge from the goddess he calls his sister.

2

NANETTE

I can't believe the dark purple bruise on Jimmy's ribs. Whoever did this is going to pay. The cut they left from the toe of their boot is deep enough that he should have had stitches and I wonder if they had a blade affixed to it to do this on purpose. I click my tongue and sigh. He should have gone to the ER.

"Jimmy, this is insane. Who did this to you?" The wound is an angry red, filled with pus. It's rimmed by the stark white of bone.

I dip the rag into the water and tear it off with a firm pull. Bubbles dance up the sides and disappear into the steam. The water is near boiling and the rag is soaked through with dark red blood. The instant I put the rag on him he screams and rips it off, splattering the water onto the floor.

"God, that hurts. Can you watch it?" Jimmy snaps at me but this is for his own good. If this thing gets infected, he'll be sorry.

"You should have told me when this happened." The water in the bowl is so soiled with his dried blood already that I'll need fresh water to finish this.

"You're just going to reopen the wound." Jimmy pushes away from me and takes the bowl, dumping the water out, and when he grabs the cloth, I try to hold onto it for a moment, but he is stronger than me. "Just give it to me, Nan. I'll do it myself."

I relent, letting go of the rag, and watch him wipe the tender skin of his ribcage until the blood is gone. The cut isn't as bad as I thought it was, though I still think it needs stitches. It will scar too, but not as bad as the scar that runs along the left side of his body. It still speaks today about the horrors we went through.

He sits back down next to me at the kitchen table, and I spread antibiotic ointment onto the wound then apply a large gauze bandage, wrapping the gauze all the way around his body so it doesn't come loose. When it's finished, I sit back and look at my masterpiece. I'm no nurse, but that should at least keep it from getting infected.

"What did you get yourself mixed up in this time?" I lean back on the old metal chair. The green vinyl is torn, evidence of a better life at some point. Jimmy is a clean man, but he holds on to the past. These particular chairs were in my parents' house before they passed away. He had to have them, said they held memories. I say they need to be thrown out like the past—forgotten and never to be remembered. I never understood how some people have fond memories and wish for yesterday. My yesterday is about as enticing as a Russian gulag.

"It's nothing, okay? You just need to stay out of this one." He pulls a shirt on over his head and then finger-combs his hair. He's hiding something, and it's probably dangerous. He does this when he's stepped across a line. He wants to protect me, but he can't. I always end up finding out and a lot of times I have to help. "I know what you're thinking, Nanette, and not this time. You're staying as far away from this as possible. You should probably leave before—"

The front door slams shut and Jimmy jumps. He swallows hard, and I see the fear in his eyes which makes my heart race too. He sits a bit straighter as we hear loud footsteps coming down the hall. I rise, hoping to cut off the unwelcome visitor and send them away, but before I get to the kitchen door, the man is here, towering over me. His broad shoulders fill the doorway, and there is no room for me to pass by him. The man's arms feel like steel as he blocks my way.

"Who are you? Why did you just walk in?" I stand with my arms crossed over my chest indignantly and he offers a half grin, as if I am a flea on a dog's back. He's intimidating, but wow is he good looking too. I don't know whether to swoon or defend Jimmy. The man is tall and broad, his body is made of ridges and valleys with swells of muscle in all the right places. His hair is a mess of dark brown waves. Though he is far, I can still smell his aftershave. It is subtle, sweet tempting. He's dressed in all black, and the only spot of color is the scarlet of his lips when he frowns at me. I have a feeling this is the bastard who gave him that boot mark.

"Tame your dog, Jimmy, before I have her removed to the sausage factory." The man's voice is buttery and smooth, a deep baritone that reverberates through me. I'm drawn to him despite my apprehension. I'm also slightly scared of him. He's huge, and he's a bit older than me, maybe ten or fifteen years. That means he's got wisdom and for Jimmy that may spell trouble.

"Look, Dom, that's my sister. She's got nothing to do with this." Jimmy trembles as he stands. He reaches for me and pulls me backward, and I go willingly. He wants to defend me; he always has. He tucks me behind his back and his head cocks to the side as he raises his hands defensively. "You can just let her go before we chat. She doesn't need to be involved."

"Ah, well Nanette here is a very priceless woman. We wouldn't want that beautiful face of hers to be tarnished. But I have some plans for her." The man—Dom? —takes a few steps farther into the room and Jimmy is cowering like a fool. I'm not afraid. I push Jimmy to the side and go toe-to-toe with the man.

"Look, I don't know what game you're playing, but Jimmy is out. You should be ashamed of yourself. Did you do that to his side? I should call the police."

"Call off your dog, Jimmy. I'm warning you." The man looks down at me, intense eyes locked on mine. Inside I'm just as scared as Jimmy, but I've dealt with his kind before and back then I was weak. I refuse to be weak. I refuse to cower again.

"Nan, please. Just let me handle this." I feel Jimmy's hands at my back, trying to pull me away but I don't back down.

"Who do you think you are?"

"Nanette, this man back here must love you an awful lot." Dom is smooth, unfussed. He hasn't raised his voice or shown even a hint of anger. Something tells me he could have assaulted Jimmy with the same placid expression on his face and never batted an eyelash. "It's because of that love that I believe you will be my greatest asset." He doesn't move, he doesn't even breathe. He's as still as a statue and twice as hard.

The familiar tremor races down my spine as I imagine his hands running down my arms, across my body. The fear of that night plagues me, but I can't let that get at me now, not when Jimmy needs me.

"Asset?" I glance at Jimmy, now nervous. What could he mean by that?

"Jimmy, have you done what I asked yet?" His eyes stay fixed on mine as Jimmy whimpers out his reply. Whoever this man is, he has Jimmy scared stiff. There's no aggression in his stare—he's like a bored and arrogant cat who knows he's the greatest parlor trick machine known to man.

"Uh, no. Dom, please. It's only been three days."

"I told you your deadline was three days." There it is, the first hint of anger. The tiniest of growls rumbles out of the man's chest and my hands are shaking as bad as Jimmy's voice.

"Dominic, please, leave Nan out of this. Let her go. We can talk when she leaves." Jimmy successfully pulls me away from Dominic and I'm glad he does. I have no idea what's happening or what job Jimmy was supposed to do for this man, but I'm scared for him now. This guy is twice Jimmy's size, and wealthy too, by the looks of it. That Armani suit wasn't cheap, and neither was the Rolex.

"What if Nan came to stay with me for a while? Maybe as a little insurance that you're going to do the job right?"

That doesn't sound like a suggestion. The tone of his voice is sinister, maniacal. His eyes drink me in like a cheap glass of whiskey. I've never had a man look at me like this before and I'm not sure if I dislike it. Jimmy stands in front of me, arms out as if building a wall. His little wall will not stop Dom, even I know that. Nothing would stop this man if he wanted something.

"No, Dom. I swear I'll do it. I swear. I just need more time, please." Jimmy is pleading now, groveling like an idiot.

"What job, Jimmy?" I ask, my voice wavering. I'm not sure if I want to know the answer.

"No, don't say a thing." Jimmy shakes his head hard. I know he's a hitman. What could be worse than that? I don't understand. He seems terrified that I'd find out what is going on, which only makes me more scared too. What has he gotten himself into?

"Jimmy, you're a smart man. I've told you that. You know how I work. I don't fuck around and play games." Dominic holds his hand out to me, wiggling his fingers. There is something in that gesture that compels me to act. I walk toward him against my better judgment, trembling the whole time. "Come on, Nanette."

"Nan, no," Jimmy pleads. He grabs my arm and pulls on it, but the gravitational force of this giant in front of me sucks me in. He's terrifying but devastatingly handsome all at once. Why do I do this to myself?

"It's okay, Jimmy. I'm going to be okay." I know if I don't go, something bad will happen to Jimmy, worse than just a boot mark on his ribs and a gash. And as much as Jimmy thinks he's been my protector for the past decade, I've been the one watching out for him. I can do this. "I'll go with you, if you promise not to hurt him again." I try to keep my tone even and my voice steady, but my voice cracks.

"Aw, look how sweet that is, Jimmy." Dominic smiles, but it's not a genuine smile of happiness. It's sinister, seductive even? "She's got your back. How devastating it would be to lose such a precious gift in your life. She's willing to fire walk for you, even though your life isn't worth the pair of boots you're wearing."

My jaw drops and the spell is broken. This man isn't charming, he's an asshole. I start to back away, but he snatches my wrist and pulls me into his side where I can't move. I push on him, grunting and clawing at his expensive suit. I want to get away. I want to take back my words, but Dominic is strong—too strong.

"The longer you take, the longer Nanette is mine. Take too long and she will be mine forever, or perhaps one of you will happen upon unfortunate circumstances." He starts to back down the hallway, clutching me to his side, and I am still squirming.

"Dominic, please. We can work this out. You don't have to do this. Please, don't do this." Jimmy follows. His hands wrap around my wrist, and he pulls but it's no use. Dominic won't ever let go. He has what he wants and I'm not sure why I am the thing that he wants.

"Finish the job, Jimmy." Dominic's last words as he forces me out the front door come with a snarl. He's angry, and now I'm alone with him. The neighborhood is quiet, but it's broad daylight. If I scream, someone will hear me. Someone will notice and call the police. But I get the feeling that if I do that, bad things will happen. I feel the gun holstered at his side, lodged into my ribcage with the pressure of his arm around my body.

"You're not getting away with this." I protest against being put in his car, pushing against the door so he can't open it, but he simply turns me away where I can't reach it, and opens it easily. "You're a monster."

"I prefer the term beast, but yes. I am. Now get in the car or Jimmy dies." He's close, too close. I can smell the leather from his jacket, the aftershave he wore. I can see the muscles in his arms flexing under his shirt.

He's stunning beyond belief, and I don't mean because of his looks. I mean because there is something so captivating and dark, something that I'm not supposed to see, something I'm not supposed to know.

His threat sobers me though. I taste the fear that dries my mouth, so thick that I can barely swallow. I glance around, hoping someone saw this, but no one is out today. Jimmy lives in too nice of a neighborhood, too quiet. Fuck. I climb into the car of my own volition and sit down. Dominic buckles me in and flips the switch in the door well to engage child safety locks. I feel the press of the seatbelt as it tightens around my waist. As soon as the door shuts, I try to open it, but it won't budge. My hand is throbbing and I'm starting to feel lightheaded.

When he climbs into the car, he reaches into his pocket and pulls out a long strip of cloth. He hands it to me as he shuts the door. "Here tie this on your eyes."

I scoff and refuse to take it. "Why?"

"Put it on, Nanette. I'm not going to ask twice." His tone tells me I should listen, though I hardly feel it's necessary. It scares me to think he could be taking me somewhere dangerous enough that I need this blindfold, but I tie it around my head, making sure my eyes are covered.

"Where are you taking me?" My hands shake as I tighten the knot and the car starts to move.

"I'm taking you where I take all my things—where they're safe. Stop asking questions."

"You don't own me, you know." I say the words, but I know they're not true. As long as I'm with him, he does own me. I know what he's expecting. A man like him gets what he wants too, and I may as well be his toy with which to do whatever he wants. The idea both terrifies me and excites me at the same time. Why does that excite me? What is wrong with me?

"I do own you, as long as your slag of a brother delays his job."

He infuriates me. I want to shout at him and make him see how abusive he's being, how he can't treat people this way, but he's armed and I'm not. And something tells me he won't hesitate to use the gun on his hip. After seeing the wound on Jimmy's ribs from the toe of this man's boot, I'm scared to death he will do something even worse next time. I can't make Jimmy do the job, so the only thing I can do is play along with this asshole and pray Jimmy works quickly.

"You're not going to hurt him anymore, right? I mean, I volunteered to come along. I need to know Jimmy will be safe." I sound foolish, pleading for my brother's safety as if I am able to bargain with this maniac. But I need reassurance. I need to know he won't hurt Jimmy.

"I said, stop asking questions."

Dominic stops the car, but he doesn't allow me to take the blindfold off. He opens my door and undoes my seatbelt, then takes my arm and walks me somewhere, up a few steps and through a door. The air smells musty, like the place has been closed up for some time. It's cool too; I shiver and rub my arms.

"Where are we?"

I hear his footsteps, then feel his fingers on the blindfold. He unties it, and as it falls away and I blink my eyes into focus I can't believe what I see. The place is a mansion, sweeping grand staircases mirrored on either side of this massive entryway. The marble floor reflects the crystal chandelier overhead. The artwork on the walls looks expensive, but everything has a layer of dust.

"You live here?" I'm gawking; I must look like an idiot. But this place is ritzier than any house I've ever been in. It's more like a castle.

"It is my home, yes, but I don't stay here often. It's... safer for you." He chooses his words carefully. "Go to the second floor, third door on the right. It is your room. There is a dress draped across the bed. Put it on and be ready for dinner at six." He turns as if he will walk away, and I plant my feet on the floor. I am not going to be bossed around.

"What I'm wearing is fine, and I'm not hungry."

Dominic rears around, a demanding glare on his face. "Let me remind you, Nanette, that if you do not do as I instruct you, your brother may not be safe." His hand draws the side of his suit coat back, revealing the weapon holstered there.

"Don't threaten me. You can't think that I am going to just be your slave, do whatever you want." I'm indignant, refusing to play this game. I'm here, and I know there are things he will expect from me, but I want to put all the cards on the table. I'm not a pushover.

He doesn't even respond. He just marches over to me and lifts me up, slinging me over his shoulder. I yelp at the sudden manhandling he does, and I realize how incredibly strong he is. I'm petite, one-fifteen dripping wet, but this guy is built. I pummel his lower back with my fists and shout. It's the only thing I can do. He's too strong to overpower.

"Stop it! Put me down!"

"Play nice, Nanette." He carries me up the stairs and down the hallway as I scream profanities at him. He walks into a dark room and drops

16

me on the bed and a squeak slips out of my mouth as I land with a hard bounce. "Dinner at six. Put the dress on and be ready."

Dominic walks out and when he shuts the door, I hear the lock click. I race over and bang on the door, screaming for him to come back, but he walks away. I hear his footsteps on the marble floor fading and I am locked in his castle to stew on my thoughts.

God, Jimmy, just do the fucking job already so I can get out of here and away from this infuriating man.

3

DOMINIC

I look at my watch—quarter past six. Nanette is late to dinner despite the fact that I sent Mika to collect her almost twenty minutes ago. I am a patient man, but when people do not do what I say promptly I do get angry. I drum my fingers across the polished mahogany, trying to keep my cool, but I'm tired of waiting. If Nanette does not come down those stairs soon, I will have to go get her and she will regret making me wait.

A door shuts, and I expect to see her enter the dining room as footsteps approach, but it is not Nanette. My maid walks in with a grimace on her face. She bows at the shoulders and nods, waiting for me to address her, but I know what she will say. Nanette is refusing to come to dinner. I can see it in her eyes. Mika is afraid of me, though she has no reason to fear me, but she is wise to know I am to be feared.

"Sir, she will not come." Mika bows again, so respectful, so I thank her.

"Thank you, Mika. I will go see if our guest will come to dinner with my coaxing." I push my chair away and stand, straightening my tie and buttoning my suit coat. "You may begin serving dinner. I will only be a moment."

She offers a pained smile and nods again, backing out of the room, and I march through the door and up the stairs. No one who really knows me would ever test me like this, so I have to be patient with her. She doesn't have a clue who I am or what I am capable of doing to her. She'll learn though, and it will only take a single interaction. She will do as I say or she will be punished, except I've reserved only the sweetest sort of punishment for a woman like her.

I approach her door and knock, but it's not latched. It swings open easily, so I push it farther and walk in. Nanette is seated casually in the armchair by the vanity, one leg crossed over the other. She is reclining, reading a magazine, and she is still wearing her jeans and t-shirt, not the dress I laid out for her. In fact, I don't even see the dress anywhere, and the room looks as if it hasn't been touched at all, except for the magazine in her hand rather than on the stack on the nightstand.

"Dinner started—" I glance at my watch again "—nineteen minutes ago. What are you doing?"

Nanette looks up at me with a dry look on her face and says nothing. Her eyes fall back to the magazine as if I've bored her or interrupted something important. One thing I hate more than being disobeyed is being ignored. I barge over to her and yank the magazine out of her hand and slam it on the vanity. The entire piece of furniture shakes, the mirror wobbling, and Nanette sits straighter in her seat.

"I was reading that."

"I was speaking to you." I don't bother trying to control my temper or my tone. I bend and look her straight in the eye. She doesn't blink or cower; she doesn't even lean away. "Get dressed, now."

"I'm not hungry. I told you that earlier." Her arms fold over her chest and she glares at me, looking me directly in the eye. I am a bull seeing red, ready to charge, and she sits there completely unintimidated by me. She clearly does not know who she is dealing with.

I will not be disrespected like this, and she is about to learn a very valuable lesson. As long as she is under my roof she will do as she is told, like it or not. I stand and fold my suit coat back, revealing my gun. Her eyes flick downward, looking at it, then back up to my face. She swallows; it's an almost imperceptible action, but I see the fear creeping into her body—shoulders tensing, pupils growing smaller, eyebrows rising.

"Jimmy has a date with the undertaker already planned out in his future. I can tell because you seem to not understand that his safety hinges on how well behaved you are."

Nanette's chin drops. Her lips purse and she grips the arms of the chair so hard her knuckles go white. I can see she is ready to negotiate with me, so I walk to the closet and find a dress that is suitable. When I walk back into the room, she is standing, arms folded over her chest again.

"I'm not wearing that," she protests, nose scrunched in disgust. She's cute when she is trying to act tough, but she will do what I say anyway.

"Put it on," I order, tossing it on the bed. It's a little blue number, open back, slit up the thigh. It is my custom to dress for dinner every night, to remember that even the devil must be a gentleman at times, and she will look good in this dress.

"I don't want to wear a dress." She shakes her head and I sit in the armchair she just vacated and watch her.

"Put it on, Nanette. I'm not asking."

She sighs and looks at the dress, then back at me. I see the anger flashing in her eyes, but she knows she has been bested. She shakes her head and rolls her eyes, then looks at the door. "Well, aren't you going to leave? At least give me some privacy to change." With hands on her hips, she waits, but I have no intention of leaving. I'm enjoying this too much, and besides she will probably not do what I tell her unless I am here to forcibly remind her, she belongs to me now.

"Get dressed, or your closet will be emptied, and your clothes will be stripped off you and everywhere you want to go, you will be naked." I lean back in the chair, ready to enjoy the show and her cheeks flush bright red. She's angry, but if I'm not mistaken, I see a hint of arousal in her eyes too. Good, I like a woman who appreciates an assertive man.

"You fucking pervert," she snaps, turning her back on me. She undresses slowly, as if she's never been naked in front of a man before, but a woman like her has definitely had some hookups. She bares her top, facing away from me, then undoes her pants.

"Face me," I tell her, my dick already tingling a little in anticipation.

"No." Her refusal only makes her all the more enticing to me.

"Turn around now, Nanette. I can't stress enough that you are mine, and you will do what I say. You can do it obediently, or you will be punished."

"You don't fucking own me, Dominic." She stands still, hands holding the fly of her jeans, and I am about to go physically turn her around myself, but she slowly pushes the denim over her hips until she is shimmying it down her thighs. The black lacy panties she wears ride up her crack a little, revealing more of her ass cheeks. They're perfect, round and perky; my hands ache to feel it, to squeeze them. She must ride dick like a pro to have an ass like that.

"Turn around, or I will make you turn around, and you don't want me to have to punish you already. It's your first day here." The silky texture of her panties is making me want to touch her more, to feel the satin smoothness of her skin.

When she turns, her cheeks are still red, and her nipples are hard. The bedroom light casts her shadow like a silhouette onto the sheets of the bed. She steps out of the jeans and reaches for the dress, and I click my tongue. "Wait," I tell her, examining her every curve with my eyes. She is perfect, tits that balance well with the curve of her hips, and I can tell she shaves her pussy too—even better. Less work for me to make her acceptable.

"Now put it on." I nod at the dress, and she does, very quickly, as if she is feeling too vulnerable or exposed in front of me. In a flash her creamy skin is covered and her green eyes glare at me with hatred. She doesn't have to hate me, but she does have to respect me.

Nanette squirms uncomfortably, adjusting the line of her panties. I stand and move toward her, selecting a pair of heels from the shoe rack just inside the closet on the way. I dangle them from one finger and tell her to put them on. As she sits, I catch a hint of her arousal wafting up to my nose. She is turned on too, another good sign. I take things when I have to, but it's easier when they're given willingly without much protest. I'll be able to pick ripe fruit from this garden anytime I want. She'll hand it over freely.

"I hate you." She straps one shoe on her foot then the other.

"I think you'll change your mind." I offer my arm and she stands.

"You are a beast, cruel and evil. I'll never change my mind." She hooks her arm around mine and I lead her to the door.

I lean down and whisper in her ear, "I smell how much you want me, Nanette. Don't lie to yourself."

We walk all the way to the dining room in silence. I own her now, and she knows it. She can't hide what her body wants any more than she can fight me. I'll bide my time though, wait her out. Fruit must be ripe before it's plucked, or it isn't sweet.

"Dinner is ready, sir," Mika says as I pull out Nanette's chair for her. She sits in it as Mika sets a plate in front of her. The wonderful scent of rosemary chicken fills the room as the lid is lifted from the plate.

Nanette's stomach growls and I think I agree. The food looks as appetizing as it smells and I'm starving.

"Thank you, Mika. That will be all." I sit as she serves my plate, and she nods and pushes her cart out the door toward the kitchen.

Nanette doesn't move. She stares at her plate as I unroll my silverware and drape my napkin over my knee. If she won't eat, I won't force her, but I'm not going to abstain simply because she's refusing food. I take a bite and moan out my enjoyment. The more I eat, the more irritated Nanette looks. She huffs and glares at me, then fidgets with her cutlery and huffs more.

"Who are you?" she asks. "And how do you have so much money? What job is Jimmy doing for you?"

I'm patient with her questions, though I don't answer a single one of them. I prefer to eat my food when it's hot, not chatter on like a ninny while it grows cold. So, I continue eating, glancing at her now and then. When I don't give her the response she is looking for, she asks more questions.

"I know Jimmy is a hitman; he's been doing that since he was nineteen years old. Just tell me what sort of hit it is. Is it dangerous? Is he going to be killed? That's why he won't tell me what it is?" She wrings her hands in her lap.

"Worry doesn't look good on you, Nanette. You're such a beautiful woman. You should smile more." I pierce a bit of chicken and bring it to my mouth, plucking it off the fork with my teeth.

"Stop avoiding my questions. I have a right to know what I signed up for." She pushes her plate away and nearly spills the glass of wine sitting next to it. I swallow my food and wipe my mouth.

"I told you in the car to stop asking questions, didn't I?" I lay my napkin on the table next to my plate. I'm content to stop eating, though I would have liked to have finished my food.

"What are you? Some sort of banker or something? How does one person own a place like this?" She looks around and gestures. "This has to be a billion-dollar home." She shakes her head, and her glare returns to me. "So, what are you paying him? And how dangerous is this? Because if he's going to get hurt, then I am leaving. I won't be your collateral. I'll tell him to—"

"Enough!" My shout freezes her in place. Her eyebrows rise, fear in her gaze.

"I just…"

"Go back to your room. I prefer to dine in peace, not with a contentious woman." My hands are fists. Her incessant questioning is infuriating. I won't answer any of her questions, and she will learn that.

"I won't. I want answers." She crosses her arms over her chest, and I see that as a clear sign of rebellion, which I will not tolerate. In a flash, I'm on my feet, stomping over to her. She fights me, swinging and kicking, but I turn her away from me, gripping both of her arms to her torso in a tight hug until her feet are off the ground.

"Fucking let me go!"

"I think you need to spend some time in your room until you learn manners. I tried to be nice, but you clearly do not get the point. You are until Jimmy does his job. You do what I say. And when I say enough questions, I mean enough."

She flails and screams as I heft her up the stairs. The way her body squirms against mine as she fights me is arousing. I briefly think about bending her over the end of the bed and showing her what it means to be punished by me but change my mind. When I pluck that fruit, it will be sweet and ripe, not fighting me and tart.

"You bastard!" she shouts, the minute the door is shut and locked. I hear her pounding on it as I walk away, but I don't heed her cries. I head to my office and park myself at my desk, watching her over the

24

closed-circuit television. The camera hidden in her room was a perfect idea. It allows me to watch her melt down, show her true colors. She is hurting, not angry. Scared, like a little waif. It's all an act. She melts into a puddle of tears, and I turn and look at the portrait of my mother on the wall.

Nanette's questions only stirred my anger. Jimmy's task must be completed, or I will never have peace. If the hit is accomplished, I will die knowing my mother was never avenged. And someone has to pay for that. The way they hurt her, the life they stole. I shake my head and reach into my desk drawer and pull out my whiskey and shot glass. After a few drinks I will calm, but now my blood runs hot. Finding out who is at the root of this plot to kill me will also uncover the truth about how they got to my mother.

I cannot die without making sure her life is avenged. So, I drink. I drink to drown that anger. I drink to calm the beast inside me. And I drink to make sure I do not go back up to Nanette's room and do something I may regret.

No, when I do that, I will enjoy it.

So tonight, I drown that beast, because otherwise, I'll lose sight of my goal.

4

NANETTE

My hand hurts. Banging on that door was a bad decision, but he has no right to lock me up like I'm a prisoner. This is so wrong, even if I did somewhat volunteer to be here. Jimmy had better do his job fast because I won't be caged up like a wild animal. I can't stand being alone. The silence is—well, I can't do it.

Tears come hard and fast, reducing me to a literal puddle. The front of the dress is damp, and I hate it. The color, the style, they belong to a far classier woman than me. I am not this woman. I wear tight skirts and leather, dark colors, not pastels and flouncy chiffon. I tear at it, ripping the thin straps right off the dress before shedding it completely and screaming. "You bastard!"

Something rises up inside of me, an animalistic urge to claw his eyes out. I tear the bedding off the bed, leaving it in a pile before turning over the nightstand. The lamp crashes to the ground in a satisfying sound and splintering glass. It only fuels my rage. "I'm going to tear apart your entire house piece by piece. You can't treat me like this. I am a human being, not an animal!"

I race over to the closet and pull the dresses out, throwing them across the room. One by one, the pastel garments fly through the air, launched by my hatred of men and my utter disgust for Dominic. He has horrible taste in women, horrible manners, and absolutely no heart. The dresses blanket the floor like carpeting, but I'm not finished. I reach up to the shelf, where stacks of slacks and jeans, still with tags on, call to me.

Each of those gets thrown out of the closet too, and then I turn my rage on the dresser. In one sweeping motion, I bring my arm across the top, scattering pictures, the alarm clock, another lamp, and a vase of flowers. Water from the vase soaks into the clothes on the floor near the dresser and the flowers spill out. If he thinks flowers are going to make me feel more at home, he clearly doesn't know me.

I turn a chair over, then eye the dresser drawers. I haven't even opened them, so I do. I find shirts and socks, panties, all in my size. All brand new. How long does he think I'm staying here? He either doesn't have any faith in Jimmy, or he is overconfident in his ability to convince a woman he is boyfriend material. Or maybe he just never intends to let me go. That thought makes me angrier.

I pull the drawers out one by one, throwing them too. Their contents scatter amongst the mess until I'm too tired to continue. I collapse onto the bed, curled up in just my panties. Even if I wanted to put on my own clothes, they've been taken. I will either have to concede and wear something he bought and put in this room, or I will have to walk around naked. Giving him the satisfaction of either doesn't appeal to me, and I devolve into more angry tears.

Only once have I been in a situation like this—where I feel powerless. And that one didn't turn out well for me. I need to get to Jimmy, to see that he's okay, that Dominic hasn't hurt him. I need to know what job he's doing, that he won't be hurt. It's my responsibility to protect him, after what happened, he needs me. He's never done this without me there, at least for advice, and now I can't even reach out to him, not a call, not a text message. Why would Dominic do this? Can't he see I'm not happy here?

I feel exposed. The anger cloaked me for a moment, but now I lie here shivering, cold, alone. I hate it. Hate how it makes me feel, like a field mouse under the foot of an elephant.

"Let me out!" I shout weakly, but there is no response from Dominic. What there is, however, is a soft knock followed by the jingling of a key at the door. I scramble, snatching up the sheet from the floor and wrapping it around myself. The door opens and the same maid who came to fetch me earlier walks in carrying a tray.

"Hello, Miss Nanette." She sets the tray down on the end of the dresser and smiles. There isn't even a hint of surprise on her features as she looks around the room. "I brought you some tea. When you didn't take dinner, I knew you'd be hungry. There are a few cookies on the tray as well."

"I'm not hungry," I tell her coldly. I shouldn't be rude because she's been nothing but nice to me, but I can't help it. I'm a prisoner here, and I just want to go home and see my brother.

"Well, the tea is nice and hot for you. I use honey to sweeten it, and a bit of cinnamon for flavor. I believe that's how you take it?" She folds her hands in front of her and I swallow back my shock. I haven't even had tea since I got here. How does she know how I take my tea? This is a testament to Dominic's reach, scary as that is.

"Thank you," I manage to choke out, but I stand frozen in place. I avert my eyes, shame washing over me. This maid will be forced to clean up the destruction caused by my tantrum, and I feel bad for her. She may even be as much a prisoner here as I am. She bends to pick something up and I glance at the door.

It stands wide open, ready for me to dart out. I know exactly how to get to the front door. It's just down the hall and at the bottom of the stairs. I know that outside, there is a flight of stairs down to the driveway; I remember that vividly though I was blindfolded. But after that, I have no clue where we are. And I'm naked. The thought of running is so tempting though, that I subconsciously take a step toward the unlocked, open door.

The maid stands, holding a white t-shirt. She clicks her tongue, and I look at her. I see sympathy in her eyes. If I'm reading her correctly, she doesn't agree with what Dominic is doing to me. It may be her soft spot, and it may be a way out of here if I leverage that.

"Miss Nanette, I know you are tempted to run, but I must warn you." Her tone is very calm and nurturing. What she's about to say, she means from the bottom of her heart with compassion—not as a taskmaster like that prick holding me here. "Dominic is a very severe man. If you try to leave here without his permission, there will be consequences, and you will not like them. It really is in your best interest to respect his wishes."

She is so convincing, in a motherly way, that I relax, prying my eyes from her comforting face to look at the open door with disappointment. She's right. I don't want consequences, not for me and not for Jimmy. I turn to her and accept the t-shirt she holds out to me.

"Do you always call him that?" I ask, letting the sheet fall. I turn my back to her and tug the shirt on, then pull my hair out of the neckline and toss it.

"What?" She bends to pick up the sheets, the proceeds to make the bed.

"Dominic? Do you always call him by his first name?" I stand back, folding my arms across my stomach. I am cold, but this t-shirt is the only thing I will permit myself to put on, and only because it was handed to me by her... Whatever her name is.

She already has the fitted sheet on, and she whips the flat sheet out, ballooning it across the bed until it settles with expert precision across the mattress. "It is his preferred name."

I take a step closer. Maybe if I know more about him, there will be a soft spot in his armor too, something I can use to get his attention, make him weak. "So, every employee calls him that? What's his last name?"

She smiles as she tosses the pillows back onto the bed and they bounce off the thick wooden headboard. "You may ask him that question yourself, dear, but I am instructed to only call him by his given name." The comforter goes on the bed as easily as the sheets, and in seconds she is preparing nurses corners to finish off her work.

So, I won't get his last name out of her, but maybe I can at least get my own clothing back. This trash he bought me isn't at all my type. If I have to be locked up, at least I can be comfortable.

"Where did you put my clothes? I need my bra and jeans... And my purse." I stand back as she walks past me, moving toward the tray of tea and cookies. She picks up the cup and smiles, walking back toward me.

"Please, try this. I made it special for you."

She smells like lilacs in the spring, and maybe a little perfume–the way my grandma used to smell each time she hugged me against her chest. I miss that old bird and her tender affection. But just like everything else in my life, she was taken from me. This woman reminds me of her, grandma, the kindness and hope in her eyes. So, I take the tea and sip it. It's delicious. She wasn't kidding. She made this tea exactly how I make it—better than I make it. Dominic did his homework correctly.

"Thank you, it's delicious."

"Your clothing has been thrown out. Dominic's orders. You have all of this," she says with a sweeping gesture. "I'm sure you'll find something you like. Just like this tea." She pats my arm and continues. "If you feel sleepy, please rest."

"But…" I realize I don't even know her name. I stumble with my words for a moment, struggling to know what to call her, and she answers for me.

"You may call me Mika."

"Mika, I don't like these clothes. I just want my own." I sip the tea again, mesmerized by how amazing it is. I've never had more delicious tea in my life.

"Dominic prefers his women to dress a certain way. I'm sure you'll adjust to it. You'll be surprised how well he knows you."

She turns and walks toward the door, and I ask, "Does he do this often? Steal women away from their families and force them to live in his castle?"

She turns and shakes her head. "He's never had a visitor like you before, though he has had a few lady guests."

Lady guests, I can only imagine that she means hookers because I can't fathom a single woman on this Earth willingly dating him. It disgusts me that he thinks he knows me so well he can sweep me away and surround me with everything he thinks I need or want only to lock me away and not even let me call my brother.

"How long will I be here?" I take a step toward the door, though her warning still rings in my head. I won't escape, not if it means consequences. He's already made it clear to me that Jimmy will die. I have to protect Jimmy; he's my life out there. The only one I have left.

"What I do know is that if you respect Dominic, he respects you. He is fair and honest."

Fair and honest? There's nothing fair or honest about him. He's a lying scumbag who takes what he wants and doesn't care about anyone or anything. I have to stifle a few cuss words that want to scream out of my throat.

"So, he hasn't told you how long I'm staying?" Maybe that really does depend on Jimmy.

"No, he hasn't. But I'm sure you'll be sleeping soon. You just rest. You can ask him at breakfast." With a wink, Mika is gone, and I am alone again, locked in my upstairs dungeon. I hear the lock click into place and I drink more of the tea. It's cool enough now, I can gulp it. It's a shame there isn't more.

I tiptoe over to the tray and eye the cookies. They look good too, like they were baked fresh just for me. Maybe Dominic doesn't know she brought them. Maybe I can eat just one of them. Despite my lie that I'm not hungry, I'm actually starving. I pick up one of the cookies, chocolate chip, and I take a nibble. They, like the tea, are perfect. I can't help but gobble it up, then another, then the third one. The tray is empty, my stomach is sated—at least for now—and I am getting sleepy.

I finish the tea and turn down the bed, still feeling guilty for making Mika do that work. Now that the bed linens are back on the bed, I notice something I hadn't noticed yet. On the floor next to the nightstand, I turned over, I see a framed image. I pick it up and study it. It's Dominic, probably when he was still teen or early twenty-something. He stands next to another man on a fishing boat. The man could be his father or uncle; they resemble each other.

He is smiling, beaming with pride as he holds a line in hand, a large fish dangling from the hook at its end. I can't imagine Dominic as a normal young man, happy and well-adjusted with normal hobbies. But this picture reveals a side of him that's softer, warmer. There is a natural shine in his eyes, like a happy boy with his family, not this beast who has me caged. What happened to him to make him become like this? Because that young man doesn't look like the sort to lock women up and treat them like slaves.

I set the image on the dresser next to the empty tray and cup, then climb into bed. It's comfortable, and slowly warms by my body heat. I stare at the photo from across the room. Dominic is very good looking. Probably the most handsome man I've ever met. Seeing a softer side of him when he was younger isn't good for my conscience. I want to hate him, stay angry with his behavior, but it softens my view of him. That image humanizes him, making me weak to his charm and understand that if I'm as fucked up as I am because of what happened to me, then maybe he has a story too. Maybe he isn't the beast I think he is.

I close my eyes, now feeling so heavy I can barely move. I yawn and pull the covers up around my shoulders and lie on my side. My mind goes back to Jimmy. I remember before my trauma, before that horrible day, Jimmy was just like young Dominic. We went to the bay and fished with Dad then too. We loved it. And when everything happened, Jimmy changed. I changed. It destroyed our family. We were never the same again after that.

Is Jimmy a monster too? Had that changed him the way Dominic changed?

No, Jimmy isn't like that.

Yes, he is a hitman, but he only takes a job when he knows the person is a really bad person who needs to die in order to let others live their life and not be harmed. He swore that to me, right after that night. That he'd never hurt anyone who doesn't deserve it.

I clung to the spare pillow, hugging it to my chest as I fell asleep. God, Jimmy, finish this job. I want to go home.

5

DOMINIC

My office is my refuge, a safe haven for my angry thoughts to swirl and multiply. Nanette can't even play nice for dinner without rousing my temper. I pour myself a glass of Johnny Walker Blue and sink into my chair. The leather squeaks as I lean back, propping my feet on the corner of my desk, and I flip on the closed-circuit TV to see if she's calmed yet. She hasn't. It's worse. She's not just banging on the door demanding to be let out. Now she's throwing things around.

And she's naked.

That fact is the one I focus on most. The camera is state of the art. I may as well be in the room with her. The way her tits bounce in her fury as she empties the closet, then the drawers, makes my dick hard. She's fiery. I like it. The anger she displays as she tears things apart reminds me of myself, the way I let loose sometimes, though not quite in the same way.

I sip the whiskey and continue watching her, thinking how sexy she'd look if she only took off those panties too. She doesn't realize that I get off on this, watching her process her trauma this way. She thinks she's destroying the room because she hates me, but I can see it in her eyes. She's punishing someone, herself maybe, for something in her past. That much rage doesn't spring up easily, and I've only just scratched the surface.

Her questions linger in my thoughts as I study her. She's very fascinated with her brother or obsessed maybe. They're closer than even I knew they were, and I want to know why. What causes her to feel the compulsion to protect him at any cost? She may not know who I am, but I've warned her enough what the consequences may be for her outbursts, and still she lashes out. Why? What makes Jimmy so important to her that she won't even sacrifice him to save herself?

Mika walks in, bringing the tea I ordered for Nanette. The TV is muted, but I see Nanette calm instantly. She is timid now. Meek? With the maid? But her eyes are on the door; she's thinking of escape. But she doesn't do it. Perhaps Mika has given her some wisdom, or maybe she understands the stakes after all.

Another gulp of whiskey goes down as the maid makes the bed and Nanette puts a t-shirt on. She looks hot in anything she wears, but those black panties and the white t-shirt set my dick on fire. It's like she's toying with me on purpose, driving me mad with lust. When she takes the tea and drinks it, I'm satisfied. Everything will be put in order while she sleeps, further proof to her that she is dealing with a powerful man.

I pull out my cell and dial Jimmy's number. Nanette isn't a handful. In fact, I want her to stay here longer, until I figure her out, but Jimmy needs to get his job done or I'm going to hurt him. Badly. The phone rings through and Jimmy answers, half-drunk maybe. His words are slurred.

"Dom... hey, I—"

"Tell me you have something." I'm not in the mood for his begging and whining. All I want is for him to finish the job so I can move on with business. Too much is riding on this, too many business deals dangling mid-process.

"Look, can't you just let her go? She doesn't have to be a part of this. She will never find out who you are or what I'm doing."

"Nanette is staying here until your job is finished, so let me know what you have, and I'll be nice to her. Or we can do this the hard way and I can mail her back to you piece by piece." I sip my Scotch again, letting the warmth trickle down my throat. I need several more drinks just to deal with him, but I don't have time to wait for them to kick in.

"Let her go, dammit! She has nothing to do with this."

"Jimmy, Jimmy, why haven't you figured out by now that I am the one calling the shots here? You remember how it felt to have my boot in your gut? Well how do you think Nanette is going to feel when she watches you take a bullet and then I finish her too?" I have no intentions of finishing Nanette off, at least not if Jimmy does his job. She's too alluring, addictive even.

"This isn't funny, Dominic. I'm going to call the police. You can't—"

"That's a very bad decision, Jimmy. First of all, you have no idea where I have her. Second of all, you have no idea who I have on my payroll. Third of all, you're likely to end up finding yourself wearing cement boots. I don't play around." I finish the whiskey and walk back to the liquor cabinet across the room and refill my glass. Jimmy is silent, so I remind him: "You work for me. And you do the job or maybe I keep your sister forever. Maybe not. Maybe she dies."

"Dammit, Dominic."

"What do you have?" With my cup refreshed, I walk back to my desk and sit down. I watch the monitor while Jimmy rambles off some useless facts. Nanette is lying down on the bed now, curled up under the blanket. She's not moving, so I assume she is sleeping or at least feeling the effects of the tea. When I've had enough of the incessant chatter, I cut Jimmy off. "Enough. Just tell me the shit I want to know."

He takes a deep breath and says, "The hit is going down soon. The man who was hired to kill you is named Alessandro Conti. Italian, notorious hitman, bad news."

The name chills me and curdles my blood. I know the man well. Too well. It's a surreal feeling, hearing that name in conjunction with a plot to end my life, given the fact that he was at the heart of how my mother died. Why she died... I squeeze the glass so hard it cracks, and before I shatter it, I set it down.

"Conti? Who put him up to it? How?" My mind reels with the information. If Conti isn't behind it, I'll be surprised, though Sven and I both know there is someone inside calling the shots too. It's possible he's gotten to someone, paid them off, offered something my father and I haven't offered. But who?

"No clue, Dom. I'm following the money. That offshore account was an alias this man uses, and he's really bad news. Like very very scary. He never makes a mistake, never misses his mark. If I were you, I'd beef up security." Jimmy is scared. Of course, he's scared. He's a pussy with a gun. Yes, pusillanimous is the exact word I would use to describe Jimmy Slater when it comes to anything mob related. But he is still the right man for the job. The only one who can weed out this mole without tipping anyone off.

"If you can follow the money to the man who is being paid, you can follow it back upstream to the account that sent it to him. Do it now. I need answers." I hang up on him before my rage can betray me, and my eye wanders back to Nanette who still hasn't moved.

Whatever this familial bond is that Jimmy and Nanette have, it goes beyond even the one I have with my brothers. We're blood, and we're close too, but we aren't that close. None of my siblings would cross someone like me to save me; of course, none of my siblings would find themselves in the same situation Jimmy is in—in my crosshairs. Still, family only means something until your blood is on the line; then you protect yourself

37

first, and family second. Otherwise, who will lead when you're gone?

Jimmy doesn't seem to understand that Nanette's existence depends on him doing his job. Nanette, however, seems to be getting it slowly. At least she didn't make a break for it when the door was open. She didn't even go back to the door after Mika left to see if it was unlocked. I instructed Mika to put the key in the lock and engage it, then disengage it. I wanted to test Nanette—see if she'd crack when given an opportunity.

She didn't.

Sighing, I unlock my phone again and call Red. He's family, but distant. He's also the only other person I can trust, though he's not the type to pull in on a job like this. I won't risk his life like that, but he can definitely help me with some fact searching.

"Yo, Dom, what's up, buddy?" He sounds happy. There is loud music playing in the background and I picture him with a few women on his lap at the nightclub.

"Red, I need information." I drink my Scotch and wait as I hear the music fading. Red is leaving the party, a wise play considering my temper tonight. But I have a soft spot for Red because he was there for me when Mom died.

"Anything, Dom. Just say the word." The music is all but gone now, faded like a ghost in the night. And Red's attention is on me.

"Nanette Elaine Slater—I need everything you have on her, as fast as possible." I stare at the monitor as she tosses. Her sleep is fraught with nightmares. It's a clue into what torment she's lived through, but I need real details, not symptoms of her internalized trauma she refuses to open up about.

"Got it… Anything in particular you're looking for?"

"Yeah, everything. I want to know where she takes every shit, you got it? And don't keep me waiting. I have my eye on her."

"Ah, I see. Dom has a new plaything," Red says, chuckling. "I'll even pull up her medical charts. I got you covered, buddy."

"Thanks, Red. Can you have that for me tonight?" One more sip and my Scotch is gone, and I'm feeling buzzed. If only I had called Red the instant I got her back here, I'd be in that room with her now instead of drinking away my urges.

"Give me an hour."

"I'll be waiting," I tell him, hanging up. Wait an hour for that priceless piece of ass? Of course.

6

NANETTE

I stir, sleep still heavy in my eyes. I should feel rested, but I don't. I feel hungover, as if I drank a bottle of tequila last night, but all I remember is the most delicious tea and cookies made by Mika. She is a sweet woman. I make a mental note to thank her for the snack next time I see her as I rub my eyes and blink them open. Sunlight streams in the window, casting a beam onto the carpet next to the bed.

For a moment I'm confused. This isn't the same room I fell asleep in, or at least, not in the same state as the way I left it. I sit up, the blanket falling off my shoulder. It's chilly, but not cold. I look around the room and see things exactly as they were when I was first locked in here. The nightstand has been righted, but the lamp is different. Maybe the other one broke when I tossed it. There is no clothing on the floor, no shoes. The dresser drawers are back in their correct places; the tea tray is gone.

Someone has been in my room while I was sleeping, and it unnerves me. I slip my feet off the side of the bed, scooting to the edge, and as the blanket falls more, I realize I'm also wearing only my panties. The t-shirt given to me by Mika last night is no longer on my body. It makes me shudder in horror wondering what happened. How did someone get into my room, clean the whole thing, take my t-shirt, and not wake me? "What was in that tea?" I ask myself aloud, rubbing my head.

"A sleep aid." Dominic's voice makes me freeze. My body instantly grows a crop of goosebumps, and my nipples go hard. I jerk the sheet up around myself and turn frantically to see him seated in a chair by the door, a chair he brought in at some point.

"How the hell did you get in here? What do you want? Why are you here?" I scoot back onto the bed, keeping myself covered. "You drugged me? You need to leave." My palms instantly grow sweaty, my heart racing. Was it him who undressed me?

"I thought you could use some help sleeping. You seemed to be a bit restless all day." He sits upright, folding his hands in his lap. One leg is crossed over the other, but he still wears the same black suit and tie. I wonder if he has even slept. He eyes me like I'm his breakfast, and I clutch the sheet around myself more tightly. "Get out. I need to get dressed."

"You may get dressed if you'd like, but I'm not leaving." He is calm but stern. I know he means what he says. It angers me, but I say nothing. There is no point in arguing with this pompous jerk. I glare at him, scooting back onto the bed. He's toying with me. "Why are your juvenile records sealed, Nanette? What happened to you?"

And now he's prying, trying to get at my weak spot. Well, I won't let him. "Get out," I scream, throwing a pillow at him. He knows nothing, and he will know nothing. I won't ever tell a soul what happened. If I do, they'll know. They'll know what Jimmy did, why he was hurt.

"I told you; I'm not leaving. And now I have questions. Like, who was it, you or Jimmy—"

"Shut up! Just shut up! Get out," I shout again, tossing another pillow at him but he merely smirks. He knows something, but I won't give him the satisfaction of confirmation. He'd have to beat it out of me. He sits there so smug, in control of his emotions like a damn robot, and all I can do is tremble. I can stand naked in a room full of strangers. That sort of transparency is easy. I understand it.

I've used my body for years like a tool. Men do what I want when I flaunt my curves. I run four times a week to make sure my body stays in prime shape too, just to keep my tool effective. But this? Dominic knowing my darkness, the pain, the wound. This is not okay. This sort of transparency isn't safe. It's scary.

Dominic stands, slipping his suit coat off. He drapes it over the chair then loosens his tie. As he slowly pulls it from around his neck, he says, "So you're going to fight me the entire way? You know I have my ways, Nanette. You think you came here simply to be leverage against Jimmy. I'm a complex man. You can't see all the things I do all the time, but in the end I get what I want."

"Stay away from me," I say, trembling. He unbuttons his shirt as he stares at me as each button is loosed. I can't pull my eyes away. His shirt opens slowly, inches at a time as his fingers work. His body is bronzed, hours in the sun or a tanning bed. His cut, well-defined muscles rippling across his chest and abs. He leaves the shirt hanging open and reaches for the corner of the sheet, just out of my reach.

I scramble, trying to hold onto it, but he tugs at it hard, yanking it from my grasp. It whips across the foot of the bed and falls to the floor, and I am left exposed, only my panties to cover me. I fold my arms over my chest. "You're a pervert. What do you get off on forcing women to fuck you?" I curl into a ball, leaning back against the headboard.

"Quite the opposite," he growls, slipping his shirt off. It falls to the floor at his feet, and he steps out of his shoes. I see the growing bulge in his slacks, and it makes my groin ache. I know what he wants, and just seeing how quickly he gets hard simply because I'm here in this bed arouses me too, but I refuse to admit it to him.

"Women get off on the fact that I even talk to them. But this isn't what it is about."

"What do you want then?" I'm not following him. He clearly wants to fuck me. His hands are working his zipper now, sliding his slacks down. His cock is hard, so long his head pops out of the waistband of his boxers. I swallow and try to look away, but he catches me noticing it.

"Don't worry, Nan. You'll get it soon enough. Just tell me, was it you or Jimmy?"

"I don't know what you mean," I tell him squirming farther across the bed. I'm at the edge, ready to fall off as he pushes his boxers down and they fall to the carpet. I know exactly what he means, and I won't tell him. I'll never tell anyone.

My pussy hurts, screaming at me to use my feminine wiles to seduce him, to let him fuck me until I'm screaming his name. Maybe that will satisfy the beast in him, and he'll let me go. I've done it before—used my body to escape like this. I just…

"Tell me, Nan. Did the judge hurt you?"

I gasp. How does he know? What does he know? I try to turn away, but he reaches for me, snatching my ankle. With one hard pull I'm supine on the bed, reaching for the far side, but his hands pin me down. "Go away!" I screech, pushing at him, but he is in my face, body pressing down on mine now. I turn my head and he breathes into my ear.

"Remember, you volunteered to come here, because you want Jimmy to finish his job safely." The low grumble in my ear sends vibrations through my entire body. I shudder with arousal. I want him; I want him so bad I can taste it. Why do I want him? What's wrong with me? He's keeping me here prisoner until Jimmy kills someone, and I'm stuck in the middle of this strange arrangement. How can I possibly want him?

"Go away," I mumble again, keeping my head turned, but he nibbles on my ear.

"Tell me your secrets, Nan. I can't help you if you don't tell me…"

His words haunt me, making me fawn at his touch. Jimmy said that, right after it happened. He said those words, and they freed me. Why are they freezing me now? Why am I here, letting this man grope my breasts? How could he possibly save me? He doesn't know what happened. He can't undo the past.

"I don't need to be saved," I snap, and look up at him as he pinches my nipple, twisting it between his finger and thumb. "You can't save me." There is a hunger in his eyes that is unmistakable. I've seen it in the eyes of a hundred men; they're all the same. He thinks he owns me.

His cock grinds against my panties and I can feel the moisture there. I know he can feel it too. A look of desire flashes in his gaze and he grinds against me again and again, a slow methodical rhythm that finds me pushing back, wanting him too.

"Someone is feeling a little aroused, aren't they?"

"Fuck you." I try to resist, but he's right. I want him. I can't fight it.

"Don't hate me, Nan. I'm only giving you what you want. I saw it in your eyes when I walked into Jimmy's kitchen."

His hands slide down my torso to the elastic of my panties and push them down. When they're around my thighs he slides his cock between my legs, letting it dip into the moisture I've made. He's thick, and long. It smears my juices everywhere and makes me clench instinctively. I hiss and grip the sheets. I want him in me so badly.

"I hate you," I whisper, whimpering as he pulls away.

"You don't hate me. You're only saying that because I own you. I know what you want, what you think, how to turn you on." He rises and tugs my panties off and I scoot back toward the headboard, but he pulls my legs back. "Stay here. Trust me, you don't want to do that. You want to obey me."

I whimper again, torn inside. God how badly I want him to fuck me, but he is the enemy. He can't do this to me, keep me here as his fuck toy while my brother does some dangerous job for him. And I don't want to want him. I want my body to fuck off, to shut down and be disgusted by him, but the instant he drops to his knees and plunges his tongue into my slit I am undone.

He eats me, sucking and slurping at my folds, growling and squeezing my hips as he scrapes his stubbled face along my thighs and groin. "Shit, Dominic…" I hiss, reaching for his hair. It's amazing the way his tongue moves across me, filling me and then pulling away. He moves his head back and forth, rubbing his nose across my clit as his tongue thrusts into me and I'm on the edge already.

I'm leaning over him, tearing at his hair and my body is on the verge of collapse. I put all my weight on his head, and he doesn't even seem to mind. It's like this is what he wants, to make me a puddling mess to control me, but this is my game; this is what I do. Not him. He is a killer, not a lover.

"Oh my god…" I lose it, clawing at his shoulders and head as he eats me. The way he hums and growls intensifies every situation until I'm convulsing, pulling his face eagerly into my pussy. I moan and scream, jerking on the bed. I've never had this, never once a man who wanted to make me feel this way. Most of them don't even care if I get off. But Dominic is not that type. It's like he gets more pleasure out of getting me off than his own release. I whine and whimper, and when I collapse back to the bed with my eyes shut, I feel his fingers searching me.

"Your pussy is tight. I need to loosen you up a bit or you're going to tear." He plunges a few fingers into me, and I have no idea what he means. I'm not tight. I've had plenty of partners, but I'm not going to complain. "Fuck, I can't wait to slide into you." He shoves another finger into my slit, and I hiss as it fills me. Three fingers hook up into me, massaging my insides, finding my g-spot.

"Oh god… oh my god," I groan. I can't reach him, so I grip the sheets again. It's so intense I may come all over him again, and the instant he presses his thumb to my clit I'm writhing.

"Yeah, that's a good girl. God, your tits bounce so perfectly when you do that." His voice drives me insane with lust. I swear if he says my name again, I'm going to lose it. No one says my name, not while they fuck me. Because no one knows my name. I'm not any man's bitch.

"Shit… Dom…" I'm panting, on the verge of begging him for it, when he leans over me, the scent of my juices on his face meeting my nostrils.

"I knew you wanted me, Nanette."

It hits me like a ton of bricks, the convulsions and spasms. I come so hard my body loses its ability to maintain control. It squirts every-where, the fluid and cum mingling as I tense, and jerk and Dominic seems to enjoy every second.

"Oh, God that's so hot. Fuck you're sexy, Nanette. Do it, come for me." His hand fucks me so hard I don't even know how his cock will compare. He slams into me, filling me and making me writhe over and over. I'm spent, exhausted already and sated, but he's not.

I sigh, melting into the mattress, and he leans over me, stroking himself. My body is weak and heavy, fully relaxed as he says, "This might hurt a bit, but I promise it will be worth it."

The head of his cock slips up and down my slit and I spread my legs to him. Just as his tip dips into me, I look up at him. He's hungry, feral even, as he shoves his dick all the way to my back wall with one thrust. I swear I feel something tear. He's massive, stretching me and filling me fuller than I've ever been.

"Oh fuck," I groan, my hands instinctively reaching for his hips as he starts thrusting. He's right. The searing pain of his cock ripping me open is replaced instantly by a pleasure I've never felt. "Oh, holy fuck."

He grunts as he thrust, leaning on the bed. His chest is inches from mine, his breath dusting across my tits making my nipples harden further. "God you're gorgeous. I'd fuck you every day if you let me," he growls, gripping a breast. And then he does something I never do. His lips brush over mine, and he nips at my lower lip.

I turn my head, but his hand moves from my chest to my chin. He turns me back to face him and stares me in the eye. What I see there scares me, but not because he's angry or hostile. It's different. It's intimate. And I can't fight it. His mouth collides with mine again and I kiss him back. I never kiss any man, but I kiss him, hungrily devouring everything he will give me.

I whimper into his mouth and clench around his thick cock as he fucks me harder and harder. I cry out in pain and pleasure until I'm so close to the edge those cries become pants and whimpers. "Now... Dom now..."

His explosion meets mine and he collapses onto me, nearly suffocating me as he slides in and out. I spasm around him, milking him as he dumps his seed into me, and he shudders when he's finished and I continue twitching beneath him. This isn't supposed to happen. I'm not supposed to want him, and I'm definitely not supposed to kiss him. He pulls out and stands. His cum slides from my body puddling on the sheets and I leap up, reaching for something, anything to clean the mess.

"Leave it. Mika will clean it up."

"She'll know we—"

"You think she doesn't know who I am and what I do?" His tone turns harsh, and I look down feeling scolded.

The magic is broken. Dominic is not some amazing man I just had incredible sex with. He's a beast. A beast who is holding me captive. I have to remember that, remind myself every time I feel a bit enchanted by him—or aroused.

But I did what he wanted. I fucked him. Now I want what I want. "Can I go now? I need to get to Jimmy, make sure he's alright."

A deep rumble of a laugh emanates from his chest, and I tense. I feel anger welling up inside me. I make fists of my hands and keep my back turned to him. I can hear him dressing as he laughs and I stand there naked, unashamed now. "You can't keep me here. I gave you what you wanted."

"You didn't answer my questions."

I whip around, ready to pounce on him, and see that he's already mostly dressed. God, he did that fast. He sits on the edge of the bed, away from the cum stain, and puts his shoes on, then stands and buttons his shirt. "You tell me what I want to know, and I'll let you go, but Jimmy stays until he does the job."

Tell him? What he wants to know? Why does he want to know it? How does he know that is the one thing I can never do? I feel tears burning behind my eyelids and I pick up one of the pillows I threw at him earlier.

"You bastard! You are such a piece of shit," I scream at him, slamming the pillow across his body. He bats it away as he reaches for his suit coat, shirt not even tucked in. "I hate you. You let me go!"

He grabs the pillow and stares me in the eye. "Play nice, Nanette or you won't get the pleasure of having my cock again."

I smack him hard across the face and he smirks at me before walking out. I'm enraged, but I listen to his footsteps on the hallway floor. He didn't lock the door...

48

7

DOMINIC

I sit in my study thinking about Nanette, wondering how she's feeling after that. I'm not a heartless bastard; I know she has to be sore. She just has a way of finding every last nerve and getting on it, maybe in part because I let her. I'm usually collected, more so than I was in the room just now, but I let her get under my skin. The closed-circuit TV shows me she is getting dressed. That's a good sign. At least she's not planning to lie in bed all day and mope.

She's fiery and mouthy, and her mouth may get her into trouble still, but for now I'm satisfied. I don't need her to tell me what happened to her. Red got me all the information I needed and after his call before first light, I know a lot more than I did when Nanette drank that tea and fell asleep. I am impressed that Mika and her help actually got the room in top shape while not waking Nanette.

I watch her as she selects her outfit and puts it on, though I admit I am disappointed to see her creamy skin disappear beneath the clothing. She's a spitfire; that's for sure, but I need a woman who is on her game. And her loyalty to Jimmy is a good thing, even if I don't yet understand it. It means if I make her mine, she will eventually be that loyal to me. A man like me needs that type of woman—secretive, faithful, and determined.

My phone rings, and I glance at it. It's Leo. He's supposed to be accepting the shipment of arms today, and he's calling me. It's not a good sign. I swipe to answer and hold the phone to my ear. "What."

"Uh, boss, there may be an issue here. We did everything you said and we're just not—"

"If you did everything I said, you would have no issues." I clench my jaw and continue. "What is the actual problem?"

"It's the guy… He's hung up in security at the gate the same way he was last time. They don't have their paperwork in order. We need you to come sign for the shipment or they're going to search the truck." Leo sounds agitated. I can't tell if he's anxious because of the potential for police involvement or if he's nervous about interrupting my morning. He should be both.

"I'm not coming down there, Leo. You and Nick have been assigned to this. You have the position you have for a reason. Handle it."

"But—"

"You heard me. Handle it." I lock my phone and toss it on my desk, irritated by the interruption. I run my hands through my hair and take a deep breath, trying to relax. But I can feel my anger simmering just beneath the surface.

As I try to calm myself down, I can feel the tension in my body, making it hard to focus on anything else. It's always the same with Leo and Nick. They're supposed to be my right-hand men, but they're always coming up short. I know that I should replace them, but they're both too valuable to risk losing altogether. And yet, every time they slip up like this, I wonder if I'm making a mistake by keeping them on board.

I try to push those thoughts aside and focus on the problem at hand. If the shipment is searched, it could jeopardize everything we've worked so hard for. And if Leo and Nick can't handle a simple security check, then what does that say about their ability to handle more critical tasks?

After a few moments of consideration, I grab my jacket and leave the office. If I want something done right, I'll have to do it myself. As I drive towards the gate, my mind still racing with thoughts of Leo and Nick's incompetence, I realize that I may need to make some changes sooner rather than later. With this whole mole situation, I don't know who I can trust either, which further complicates things. I'm halfway to the yard when I get another call. This time it's from Jimmy. I take a deep breath before answering, bracing myself for the news he's about to deliver. "What?"

"Dom, the hit is going to go down at the yard—today. They're coming for you. They have their hitman undercover as a security guard. They're waiting for you to show up."

My stomach churns at his words. This is it. The hit has finally come. I've been waiting for this moment for weeks, ever since I found out that someone had put a price on my head. I still don't know who hired the man though, and that's the real information I need.

"Who hired him, Jimmy?" I am enraged as I turn the car around, heading back home. "Because that is what I hired you to find out."

Jimmy stammers out a few nonsense words. I'd like to choke the man, though I try to keep tabs on my temper since he did just save my life.

"Dom, it's not that easy," he mumbles.

I grit my teeth, fighting back the urge to scream at him. "Make it easy, Jimmy. That's why I pay you."

"I know, boss, but it's going to take some time to get that kind of information. Maybe a few weeks at least."

51

I swear under my breath, feeling trapped and vulnerable. I can't show up at the yard right now knowing that a hitman is waiting for me. And I can't stay away for too long because that would raise suspicions and put me in danger of being found by whoever wants me dead. "What do you mean it's not that easy? You've had weeks and yet you still don't know who put a hit on me?" I bark into the phone. "I paid you good money for this information, Jimmy. You better have something more concrete than 'it's not that easy'."

"I'm sorry, Dom, but I've hit a dead end. The guy who hired him is using an encrypted messaging service to communicate. I can't hack into it no matter what I try," Jimmy admits, his voice trembling with fear.

I take a deep breath and let it out slowly, trying to keep my temper in check. "Alright, fine. Just keep trying. If you find anything else, call me immediately." I hang up and toss the phone onto the passenger seat next to me.

Now, on top of everything else, I have to worry about losing my shipment. This damn mole is costing me dearly, and I don't even know who it could be. I grind my teeth in frustration but force myself to stay focused on the task at hand.

As I pull into my driveway, I reach for the Glock 19 tucked in my waistband. It's been a while since I've had to use it in self-defense, but better safe than sorry. With a deep breath, I steel myself for what's to come and step out of the car.

I make my way toward my study, sinking behind my desk again. To think I came this close to dying and someone within my organization is the one who set me up is infuriating. If I were a weaker man, it would make me cower, fall to my knees and hand over my throne. But I'm not a weak man. I'm a beast, trained to hunt down the bastards who think they are smarter than me. Is it Leo or Nick? They're my right-hand men, but neither of them would get my spot being in charge of the family. And I just can't believe one of my brothers would do something like this; we're blood.

I lean back in my chair, deep in thought. The mole has to be someone I least suspect, someone I trusted completely. But who? I rack my brain, going through every possible scenario in my head. I need to find out who's responsible for hiring that hitman before they try again. My first thought is to interrogate Nick and Leo. If I do that, however, I'll play my hand too early. If one of them is the mole, they'll tip everyone off and we'll have a war. If I take out the hitman, a new snake will arise in his place and the mole will know we're on to him.

"Dammit!" I growl, slamming my fist down onto my desk. This is what I paid Jimmy for, and he better come through. My eyes catch a glimpse of Nanette on the closed-circuit TV again, leaving the room. This thing got a whole lot messier when I dragged her into it, but I'm not about to give her back. Not now. Not since I know how to make Jimmy do what he's told.

8

NANETTE

I found my way to the kitchen without help, the scents of bacon and coffee luring me out of my room. Now I sit across the island from Mika, watching her plate a breakfast made for a king. I didn't say anything when I came in, but she didn't either. I like that we can have companionable silence. I'm not necessarily a morning person, so not having to talk to her is a good thing. She slides a plate of eggs and bacon in front of me then hands me a fork, after which comes the cup of coffee. She busies herself working on cleaning up and I dig in.

I feel like I haven't eaten in weeks; I'm starving. The cookies last night were a great snack, but I'm thankful she can cook more than just cookies. I empty the plate quickly and she notices. "More breakfast?" she asks with the pan in hand, ready to fill my plate again, but I shake my head. If I'm going to keep my figure at this place, I need to practice the same self-control I have at home. Especially since I'm not able to run here. "Suit yourself," she says, scraping the pan out into the garbage disposal.

I sip my coffee, feeling the heat of it warm me from the inside out. I want to ask her how long she's been working for Dominic and find out what she may know about him, but I hesitate. She wasn't exactly forthcoming when I asked her about him last night. I'm not sure what protocol is in this house and the last thing I want is for him to lock me up again.

"Dominic told me when you first got here that if you were obedient to him, he would let you have freedom in the house. I'm happy you don't have to be locked up anymore. That is an awful way to live," Mika says, clicking her tongue.

I wonder if she had to be obedient to him too, or if she knows what "being obedient" meant to him. I look down into my half-empty cup of coffee and try to hide the embarrassment turning my cheeks pink. I'm ashamed to admit I liked being obedient to Dominic.

"You should go out to the garden this morning. The songbirds are singing and it's so beautiful out." Mika absently washes dishes while she talks but I'm not fully listening. My mind is elsewhere, in that bed with him while he did those incredible things to me. Things I want him to do again.

"Oh, and you should visit the library too. Dominic has so many wonderful books."

Her words pique my interest. "Books?" I take another drink of the coffee and realize it's getting cold. There's nothing worse than cold coffee, so I push it away and stand, smoothing my hands down the front of my jeans. "Where is the library?"

Mika's hands are buried in the water, but she nods at the door. "Down the hallway on the left. You'll see it." I start toward the door, and she adds, "Don't go into any other rooms though. You will find yourself getting locked up again. Just a friendly warning from one woman to another."

Her warning is noted, and I walk out into the hall and wander away from the kitchen. The ornate wood carvings on every door frame speak of history and money. This place has to be over a hundred years old. Every single surface is decorated with some sort of art, telling stories of historical figures and events. The way Dominic has had this preserved is almost majestic. I find myself being drawn to a specific door, where a woman's face is etched into the wood with so much detail, it comes alive, watching me move.

I am fascinated by the artistry, and I wonder if there is more on the other side of the doorframe, so I try the knob and find it unlocked. I push into the room, studying the intricate carvings on the frame, and a portrait on the wall catches my eye. It is a beautiful woman, painted in Victorian fashion, but she looks modern, with striking blue eyes— eyes that remind me of Dominic's. Her hair is swept to one side, framing her heart-shaped face, and her smile mesmerizes me. I swear I've seen this woman before somewhere, but I can't place the face or the image anywhere.

It's not a historical painting; I don't recognize the name of the artist scrawled on the bottom right corner of the piece. But the more I study it the more I'm convinced that I do know this woman. I step closer to get a better look, almost ready to touch the picture, as if that will give me some connection to her—a way to discover who she is simply because of proximity to this art.

"What are you doing?" Dominic's voice booms from the doorway and I freeze. I swallow hard remembering what Mika said. I should have stayed out of here, but I am too curious. I was only looking at the art. "You shouldn't be in here." Dominic is angry, enraged almost.

I spin around to face him and see his face contorted in an angry scowl. "I…" I utter, hoping to protest, but he is on me, racing toward me at lightning speed. His hands grasp my arms, and he shakes me hard twice.

"Who gave you the permission to come in here?"

I jerk away from him, terrified by this sudden outburst of rage, but I don't let on that I'm scared. "It's just a bedroom. I was looking at the art!" I step away from him, nervous about what he may do to me. I've never seen him this angry. A vein bulges across his forehead, his eyes bugging out. His face is red too, and his hands are fists at his side. Why is he so upset over me looking at this woman? Who is she?

"You are a guest here, and guests are supposed to mind their manners, not go snooping."

"Who is she, Dom? The woman in the painting." I try not to cower, but he grabs my wrist and forces me toward the door against my will. I whimper and try to twist my arm out of his grip, but he holds me so tightly I'm certain it will leave a mark.

As he pushes me into the hallway, I stumble and nearly trip, trying to keep my balance. My heart is pounding in my chest, beating so fast I'm afraid it will burst through my ribcage. I take a deep breath and try to calm myself down, but my mind is racing with questions.

"Who is she?" I ask again, trying to get a better look at Dominic's face. He doesn't answer, just continues to glare at me with his cold, hard eyes. I can't tell what he's thinking, whether he's angry or scared or something else entirely.

"Why won't you tell me?" I plead, reaching out for him. But he steps away from me, his hand still gripping my wrist tightly.

"You have no right to be in this room," he says through clenched teeth. "And you have no right to ask questions about things that don't concern you."

"But she does concern me," I say softly, looking up at him with pleading eyes. "I don't know why, but I feel like I know her. Like she's important somehow."

His grip on my wrist tightens even more, and I wince in pain. "You don't know anything," he growls, pushing me harder into the hallway. "Now get out of my sight before I do something we'll both regret."

I stumble backward again, feeling tears prickling at the corners of my eyes. I refuse to cry in front of him, to let him see me as weak. He locks the door and when he turns, he glares at me, as if he expects me to have vanished. "I don't want you asking about her again!" he warns, his voice low and menacing. His eyes are bloodshot, and I can't help but feel scared.

"I'm sorry! I just wanted to know who she was..."

"You don't need to know anything about her," he growls. "Now go back to your room and stay there until I say otherwise." His grip on my wrist loosens a bit and I try to pull away from him, but it only makes him angrier.

"Don't try to fight me, Nanette," he warns, his breath hot on my face, making me shiver. "I'm the one in charge here, and you do as I say." He leans closer to me, his face only inches from mine and I realize how tall he actually is. His scent fills my nostrils and it's a mix of musk, leather, and spice. It's intoxicating.

"What are you going to do?" I whisper, not really expecting an answer.

"Nothing if you do what you're told." He releases his grip on me completely and takes a step back. "Now go."

Something stirs inside of me. He's hiding something from me, something he doesn't want me to know anything about, and it has to do with that woman. My mind races, trying to think of where I've seen her before, because if I can figure out who she is, I may just have leverage over him, enough to get me and Jimmy out of this situation.

"Why won't you tell me who she is?" I ask, stepping forward and his hand comes sweeping across my face. The back of his knuckles connects to my cheek in a hard blow, though I'm more speechless than hurt.

"Is that what you like, Nanette? You want men to abuse you? You like it rough?" Dominic moves toward me, a large predator cornering his prey. "You like to be bossed around? Does that work you up? Is that why you do what you do?"

I swallow hard, pressing my back against the wall behind me. He's in my face, breathing down shirt. He doesn't touch me again, but the thrill of him pursuing me like this does things to me no other touch could ever do. He's right. I'm so screwed up this is a turn on. Most women would be terrified of this, a huge man his size with anger in his eyes advancing on them. But not me. No, my past fucked me up so badly, this is what turns me on, gets me going.

"Shut up!" I scream, pushing my hands against his chest, but he doesn't budge. How does he know? Why did he say that? Does he know what I do? What sort of connections does this man have that he can find information on me that I try to bury, to keep secret even from Jimmy?

"That's it, Nan. Resist me. Is that what you do? You play the victim so the men you sleep with will become the aggressor just so you can get off? Are you a masochist too?"

I push on his chest again and he captures my wrists in one of his massive hands. "You know nothing." I spit in his face, and he chuckles a deep sinister laugh. He's evil, pure evil. I can see it in his eyes. He's done bad things, horrible, unspeakable things, and I may be his next victim.

"I know more than you think."

"You know nothing," I shout, pushing against his grip, but he is strong. "You're a monster. What horrible things have you done?"

Dominic licks my cheek, then bites it and I shudder. It sends a jolt of arousal through my body. I want to fight, but I can't. My core tightens, aching and producing a puddle in my panties.

"You think I'm bad, Nanette, but you're just as bad. You've done very bad things," he whispers, and I hold my breath as his knee slides between my thighs. "You like it rough, Nanette? Like to have men rough you up a little? Does it help you get off?" His knee grinds against my mound and I whimper.

59

"Shut up!" I hiss, but he doesn't stop.

"Does it make you feel powerful, or do you just have a death wish?"

"Shut the fuck up, Dominic!" I scream shoving at his chest the instant he lets my hands go, but God do I want him. When he covers my mouth with his, I forget about the woman in the painting, or the anger in his eyes. All I can do is give in to him—again. He's right. It's a sickness inside of me, to let a man treat me how he wishes. The rougher the better, the more demanding and angrier, the harder I get off, and here I am tearing at his clothing because I need it now, again.

9

DOMINIC

I pin Nanette to the wall, claiming her lips as mine. Lips are for love, and I never do this with any other woman, but she has me by the balls, literally. Her hand is down my pants groping me. She wants this as much as I do, and I'm not sure if I want to give it to her like this. But my body has a need. After the shock dealt to me this morning, I can't refuse her.

"You want this, don't you?" I growl in her ear, pressing my body close to hers.

She nods, gasping for breath as I continue to kiss her neck and collarbone. I slide my hand up her thigh, feeling the heat emanating from between her legs. I yank her jeans down her hips until they're bunched up around her knees. Her panties are already damp, and I can see the outline of her clit through the fabric. I rub my thumb over it through the lace, feeling her shudder in pleasure. My own cock is straining against my pants, and I release it from its confines, stroking myself as I tease her.

"You like that?" I ask, rubbing my thumb harder and faster until she's grinding against me. "You want more?"

She nods eagerly, and I push her panties aside and slip a finger inside her without warning. She's so wet that it slides in easily, and I curl it up to hit that sweet spot inside of her. Her breath hitches in her throat as she clings to my shoulders for support.

"Please," she begs, and I know what she wants.

I pull out my finger and rip off her panties with one swift yank. She gasps at the sudden exposure, but before she can say anything else, I'm pulling my dick out and burying myself inside of her. It's been a while since I've had rough sex like this, but Nanette brings something out of me that no one else can, a beast that needs sated.

"You like it rough, don't you? You need it to get off. Admit it," I order, ramming my cock into her tight hole. She tears at my shirt, opening it in the front. Her hands glide over my flesh, scratching at my skin.

I pound into her relentlessly, listening to the slap of flesh against flesh as she moans and cries out. Her pussy is tight, and I know that she's getting closer to orgasm by the muffled cries she's making under her breath. I want to hear her scream, so I deviate from my pattern and fuck her in a different angle, striking a thicker wall inside of her that has Nanette crying out in pleasure. Her body is on fire, and she explodes into an orgasm that leaves her trembling and gasping for air, clinging to my shirt like it's a lifeline. The walls of her pussy clamp down around my cock, and it takes all of my self-control not to follow her into release.

The moment passes, and she sinks against my chest from exhaustion, but I'm not finished. I want more from her; I want to hear her scream my name. So when I pull out, and she thinks it's over, I flip her around and grab her hips in my hands. I bend her over, accessing that deep well from behind. Before she can complain, I plunge back into her. She moans, and I continue relentlessly as I reach up her shirt and play with her tits. Her bra is in the way, so I pull it down, pinching and teasing her taut little buds until she's begging for mercy. She's magnificent like this, all flushed and ready for me. But I want even more, so I smack her ass for good measure. It leaves a red handprint on the pale white skin, and before long it's glowing from my abuse.

"You're a bad girl," I whisper in her ear as she moans in surprise and pleasure. "Tell me what you are."

"I'm a bad girl," she says breathlessly.

"And what do bad girls need?"

"They need to be punished." Her voice is low and throaty with desire, but she speaks the truth. I'm on the edge, but I slow my thrusts, making sure I don't go yet. Her ass is too tight, too perfect to go that quickly. I grind into her, sliding in and out as she whimpers and pants.

I reach down and grab a fistful of her hair, pulling her head back to expose her neck. "You're mine," I growl into her ear.

She moans in response, and I kn0w then that she's going to be trouble. But damn if I don't love a good challenge.

Her muscles clench around me as I continue my slow pace. I revel in the feeling of her warm body against mine, savoring the sweet torture of teasing her. Her back arches as she tries to push back into my thrusts, but I hold her hips firmly in place.

"You want it harder?" I growl, my voice thick with lust.

"Yes," she gasps, and she clenches. It sends a shockwave through my body. I give in to her plea, increasing the force and speed of my movements. Her body jolts with every thrust, her moans growing louder and more urgent. I reach around and slip a finger inside her, syncing it with the rhythm of my thrusts. She cries out in pleasure as I hit that spot inside her that drives her wild.

"That's it," I whisper, my own release just within reach. "Come for me." Her whimpers grow more intense. I feel her hand as she massages her clit, competing with my ministrations. She likes it in both holes at once. That's hot. "You're mine," I growl into her ear. "Say it."

"I'm yours" she pants, and I push her fingers away from her clit as I straighten.

"Louder." I fuck her harder and faster. She gets louder with each word, until she's screaming, "I'm yours, I'm yours" over and over again. Her body is shaking with pleasure, and I know it won't be long for me. Her sopping wet pussy almost feels like heaven on earth against my cock.

Her noises are spilling over into the quiet apartment complex, but neither of us care. Her orgasm is coming, and I can feel my own building up. Her walls clench around me as I slap her ass again, watching it redden more as she cries out. Even through the pain, she still wants more of me. She mistakes my pause as hesitation, so she reaches back behind herself to grab my dick and pull it toward her dripping hole, rubbing it up and down the slit until the precum makes it easier to slide into her entrance than anything else would. It takes me a moment before I regain control over myself, but then I'm ramming against her ass cheeks forcing myself deeper inside of Nanette than ever before. Her cries of delight fill the hallway as we fuck with abandon.

I reach under her and decide her clit is mine this morning. I tease, flick and pull it until she's begging me to stop. I don't know if I could; this feels too good. Her legs begin to shake, but I don't give her a chance to rest as I continue my onslaught of her softness, filling the nooks and crannies until she's grinding back against me wanting more.

"Oh God!" she screams, and I know that she's right on the edge of another orgasm. I go faster, fucking her faster until she is almost there.

"You're so close," I whisper in her ear, and then I bite down on it, hard. That's what sends her over the edge, and she moans as her climax overtakes her body, causing her to shake and tremble in ecstasy. I push into her once more, deep and hard, and she comes undone with a low cry.

She suddenly stiffens and cries out as another orgasm shatters through her body. Her thick muscles clamp down on my dick like a vice grip, milking my cock for all it's worth. With one final thrust, I come too. My body shakes with the power of it, my seed shooting inside of her so hard that there is no way for her womb not to take it all in. She moans softly and collapses against the wall as I slide out from behind her. I pull up my pants, watching her shudder on the floor like a puddle I just splashed in. It's intoxicating knowing I did that to her.

She straightens up and fixes her bra, looking a little ragged around the edges like she just went through hell. I reach down and yank her jeans off the rest of the way, her sandals dropping to the floor. She whimpers and tries to fight me, but I am stronger than her. I hand them to her, dangling them from a finger, and she glances at the torn panties on the ground next to her.

"Why did you do that? We're done," she asks, snatching her shoes and panties into her hands. There is a look of disgust on her face, but I can tell there's something hiding behind.

"Because you didn't say thank you," I respond, shrugging slightly.

"What?"

I cross my arms in front of me, daring her to disobey me. She stares at me gritting her teeth. It has to be embarrassing being undressed in a hallway, but what's done is done. "Go ahead and take your panties; you're welcome."

"And you're an ass," she says, beginning to put her pants back on.

"No," I tell her sternly. "Go to your room."

Her eyes meet mine in a defiant look, but she says nothing. She moves toward the stairs, shoulders hunched over. This is part of the lesson she's learning, to obey me no matter what, and maybe I get some satisfaction out of watching her walk the hallway half naked with my cum dripping down her thigh. The curve of her ass and the cherry evidence of my hand on her ass cheek bring a smirk to my face. I trail her up the stairs, noticing how she glances around to make sure no one is watching.

"Don't like being exposed? Don't want people to see you?" I ask her, and she peers over her shoulder.

"Fuck you."

"I know who you are, Nanette. I know what you do."

She swings the door open to her room and slams it as I enter, but I catch it, stopping it from hitting me. She thinks she's going to get away from me, but she doesn't know who I am, the lengths to which I will go to make sure she understands I'm in charge. I gently shut the door after entering, then sit in the chair I occupied this morning.

"You know nothing." She walks straight to the nightstand and collects a few tissues from the box, cleaning the evidence of our sex from her body.

"How many men in this city have you fucked? The governor? The city commissioner?" I watch as she tosses the tissues away and drops the sandals. She carries her jeans to the dresser where she pulls out a pair of clean, not torn, panties.

"My personal life is none of your business, you bastard."

"Beast, I told you. I prefer it."

Nanette drops the jeans, bending to put her legs into the panties' leg holes, but I click my tongue. "No. You're not dressing now. Sit on the bed."

"You can't do this to—"

"Sit on the bed, Nanette," I order, and she complies. "Spread yourself like a good girl."

She rolls her eyes at me, but she obeys, spreading her legs so I can see her sweet pussy on display. "That thing has fucked a lot of men. I'm surprised you're clean."

"How do you know!" she hisses, closing her legs.

"A high-class escort doesn't stay a secret long in my world."

As the words slide out of my mouth she cowers. "Please, let me get dressed. Please, Dominic, I don't like this."

I stand, buttoning my shirt. "We're going to dinner. You will behave yourself or your brother won't see the light of day. Do you understand?"

She nods, scrambling for the panties. As she slips them on, she asks, "The scar... on your chest. How'd you get it?"

I pause, head down, facing away from her. "Only the beautifully broken get to see the beast with his mask off."

I leave her locked in the room, unable to answer that question. It's too real, too raw. She had to go there, poke at my wounds. It drives me straight to the room I just chased her out of. I need to see that portrait, to feel that pain again. It fuels me, reminds me why I'm doing what I'm doing. My mother needs avenged. It isn't right what they did to her, how they hurt her.

I enter the room and stare up at the painting, wishing I had a glass of whiskey. Nanette had no business in here, seeing this. Some things are meant to be kept private, treasured. This room is just as Mother left it, untouched except for the bloodstain on the floor by her dresser. I scrubbed that with my own hands. I look there, knowing how she was found, how I found her. It isn't right.

Rage bubbles up in my chest and I slam my fist against my thigh. Punishing myself won't help, but it gives me an outlet. I take a deep breath, stepping closer to the portrait. It's been years since I've looked at it properly. The last time was at Mother's funeral when I had to give the eulogy. I remember staring at it then too, trying to pull together all the good things I could say about her.

But now, standing alone with her painting, I allow myself to truly look. It's eerie how much we look alike. Her brown hair is like mine, her small nose, and thin lips. In this portrait, she wears a blue dress that brings out the green in her eyes. I had no one else after she was taken from me, and now everyone will pay for what happened.

I let out a deep breath and take a step back from the painting before turning to leave the room. As I pass by her dresser, I catch a glimpse of something that makes me pause. It's the letter I found next to her. My head tilts to the side as I approach it, and I pick it up to read what's written on it in my mother's delicate script.

"My dearest Dominic,

If you're reading this note, it means I'm no longer with you in this world. But please don't cry for me, my love. Know that I'm at peace now and free from the pain they caused me.

I want you to know that I never stopped thinking about you, even in my darkest moments. You were always my light in this world. Please don't let their cruelty dim that light, my darling. Live your life to the fullest, and make sure justice is served.

With all my love,

Mother"

Tears prick at the corners of my eyes as I read her words, feeling a mixture of sadness and anger wash over me like waves crashing against the shore.

"I won't let you down, Mother," I say to the empty room before tucking the note into my pocket and leaving.

1 0

NANETTE

I spend much of the day in my room, though I did go to the kitchen for lunch. I had a nap, but I feel fatigued this evening as I dress for dinner. Mika told me which dress I had to wear—orders passed on to me from Dominic. I hate the way he makes me feel like I'm a slave, only here to do his bidding. But I like it too.

The dress is pleasant enough, pastel purple with ruffles on the thin straps. The bodice fits perfectly. It's like he had these dresses tailor made for me. Like he knows my measurements by heart, simply by looking at me. He doesn't; he can't. No man is that smart or that connected. And even if he is, who does he think he is to select clothing for me that I'd never wear if I were the one picking things. It's like he's trying to soften me or something. I don't need to be softened. This world made me tough, and that's who I am now. I need that edge or I'll…

I stand in front of the mirror reflecting on the morning, the way Dominic made me feel. His knowing doesn't stop at my clothing size. It's like his hands know exactly how I like to be touched. Like intuitively he maps my body and memorizes it, then follows the map like a guidebook to bring me to the precipice of ecstasy only to plunge me into the depths of orgasm time and again. But why does he care?

I'm damaged, a wrinkled suit—Pandora's box. What I hold inside is toxic and if he opens the wrong door, I'll bleed blackness onto his soul. But it's like he wants it. He wants a broken girl who needs to be abused to get off. Rich, powerful, older men are the ones I choose, probably because I was abused by one. He got in my head, ruined me. Now it's my type, and I hate it. The men I seek out aren't men anyone should desire, but here I am this sick little waif, fawning over them until they spoil me with their lust. It's not like I have a choice anyway. I chose being an escort because I have no skills, no education. It pays well, and it meets a need I have—sometimes.

Pushing away the thoughts, I fluff my hair. I like it down, but I know Dominic probably does too. So I put it up. He hasn't put any pins or clips in my room, so I twist my hair around in a knot until it's piled on my head and tied to itself. A few stray hairs frame my face and I think it looks elegant. After a splash of makeup, I'm ready to go out to dinner.

Dominic said Jimmy would be there, so I'm looking forward to seeing him. I know I'll have to "play nice" as Dominic says, but at least I get to see him, to make sure he's okay. When I bandaged the wound on his side he appeared to be in a lot of pain. I hope he went to the ER and got stitches. Dominic did a number on his ribcage. And this job, whatever it is, he needs to finish it so I can get out of this damn house. I want my life back and it's only been two days.

Someone knocks at the door, and I turn to see Dominic standing there in a black tux. He looks incredible, hair parted to one side but still dangling across his dark, brooding eyes. He hasn't shaved; it seems to be his signature look, the five o'clock shadow. His eyes scan me, as if looking for fault or defect. It isn't the sort of examination a man gives you when he's aroused by you, just a cold, hard stare for quality purposes. I feel like a toy being examined before purchase;

except I know he has no intention of doing any purchasing. Just playing with me for free.

"Are you ready?"

I nod, turning back to see my reflection one last time. I feel put together even if I don't like the way he makes me dress. When I spin back around and head for the pair of strappy, silver heels, he clicks his tongue and I look up at him.

"Is that really how you're wearing your hair?" His brows furrow and I roll my eyes.

"Yes, it really is." I pick up the heels and put them on and he doesn't say another word, though I can tell he isn't quite happy about my hair. That, of course, makes me happy.

He leads me out into the hallway then down the stairs. A car is waiting for us as we exit the place. I am naïve, thinking we will just get in the car drive to the restaurant where we will have dinner, but the minute we are in the car, he reaches into his pocket and pulls out a hand-kerchief.

"You know the drill," he tells me. At least this one is made of softer fabric, and on the upside, I have my hair up so it won't be messed up. I tie the thing around my eyes and sit back as the car starts moving. My mind is already swimming with questions I want to ask Jimmy. I wonder if Dominic is going to be angry when I ask them, but I am not an arm piece just to be viewed. I will speak my mind if and when the opportunity presents itself.

"Where are we eating?" I ask.

"A family restaurant, you'll like it." He speaks with authority, as if he knows my likes and dislikes. He's too cocky. Someone needs to take him down a notch or two. A man like him has resources, sure, but they are limited. Maybe he knows where I live, what I do for a living. He may even know what happened to me—it's not like there was no news coverage of what happened to Jimmy. He's smart; he'd put the pieces together. But my likes and dislikes?

"You're Russian? What are you planning to feed me? Borscht?" I scoff, knowing I absolutely hate borscht. If he could see me, he'd see me rolling my eyes again.

"No, I plan to order you the *okroshka* with *pelmeni*." He says it with such confidence I can only believe he really thinks I will like it. It satisfies my frustration strangely, and I change the subject.

"Have you hurt him?"

"Who?" Dominic plays stupid. He knows exactly who I'm talking about.

"My brother. Have you hurt him? Will I have more gashes to his ribs to bandage up?" I use a tone that communicates my disgust for his force. Jimmy is a tender soul at heart. I never have to do much more than give him a look and he listens to me—a grown man older than me and still listening to his sister about things like stray cats and water dishes.

"Jimmy is fine if he does his job." Dominic clears his throat and I hear the leather of his seat squeak. "If you cause trouble tonight, there is a bullet with his name on it, though. How do you like that?"

I bite my tongue. I want to lash out and tell him what an ass he is, but I know that will only incite his anger. As much as I like angering him, I want him to be calm so I can enjoy my time with Jimmy.

The rest of the car ride is silent and when Dominic reaches over to remove my blindfold, I blink my eyes open to see we are in the heart of New York City. If I didn't grow up around here, I'd be craning my neck like the tourists. These buildings are old news to me, though, and I just want to get to the restaurant. So, when the car stops, I hardly wait for the driver to walk around and open the door.

"Shall we?" Dominic asks, holding out his arm to me, and I rest my hand on it. He leads me through the front door of a Russian place. I can't even read the name, let alone pronounce it, and everyone is speaking what sounds like babbling to me. I smile and nod when a polite woman says something to me as the hostess stand and follow her and Dominic as they weave through tables. The one she leads us to is in the center of the room, surrounded by dozens of other patrons.

Jimmy is waiting. He stands to greet me, offering a hug. His hands slide down my arms to my hands where he squeezes them. He looks into my eyes. "Are you okay? Is he treating you well?" Jimmy asks in a whispered flurry of words.

"We should sit," Dominic says sternly, holding his tie against his chest. I nod, not wanting to anger him. There will be time enough to enjoy catching up while we dine.

Jimmy gives me a nervous look, but he nods too, and we sit, followed by Dominic.

The restaurant is quiet despite the masses gathered here eating. White linens adorn every table, with silver flatware and black cloth napkins. This isn't a cheap place, though with Dominic's money, I hardly think he ever eats at what I would consider a cheap place. Even the waiters wear full black-tie apparel. Ours approaches and Dominic orders in Russian, another jumble of unintelligible words. When the waiter is gone, he turns to Jimmy.

"Any news yet?" Dominic snaps his napkin out and drapes it over his lap. I sit nervously, waiting for my opportunity to speak to Jimmy without causing a stir.

"Maybe, I'm following a lead. More ties to the Italian fellow, and a potential trace back to you. I have to be certain and I'm waiting on a source." Jimmy speaks with Dominic in a confident tone, though I know it's an act. That's not my Jimmy, not after what happened. Not even the fancy suit he's wearing could give him that amount of confidence. He sure is a good actor though; should have been on Broadway.

"Good, I need that report as soon as your source relays the information." Dominic nods at an approaching waiter who has two wine glasses, a bottle of wine and a beer. He sets the beer in front of Jimmy —some sort of rye malt called *kvass*. He even knows Jimmy, which is beginning to concern me.

The waiter sets one wine glass in front of me, and one in front of Dominic and fills them to the brim, then nods, smiles and walks away without words. I watch Dominic elegantly pick up the glass and sip from it, though I won't do the same. I want a clear head. I turn to Jimmy as Dominic has his drink.

"How are you feeling? How are your ribs?" I want to reach out and touch him, grab his wrist and hold his hand while we talk. I'm worried about him, but I don't dare anger Dominic.

"I'm fine. The wound is healing. Just have to get to business now."

"You don't have to do this, Jimmy. It's very dangerous." I reach for him, and Dominic clears his throat. The way he adjusts his coat reveals the Glock holstered against his chest under his arm. I swallow hard and sit back, nervously picking up my wine glass without thinking. I take a sip as Dominic speaks.

"The job will be done, and I warned you not to cause a scene, Nanette. You're here for one reason only." He closes his coat and leans forward with a sinister smile on his face. I don't know what purpose he has in bringing me to dinner with him and Jimmy if I'm not allowed to speak my mind.

The wine is good, and strong too. After only a few sips I am feeling a tingle in my neck and shoulders. I hate that it's so good because I don't want to get drunk, but I want to drink more. Jimmy and Dominic dive off into a conversation about things I don't understand. It's mostly code talking but I know they are speaking about the job. I try to distract myself by studying the room, but the people here seem pretentious. Not at all my crowd. Their pinkies are in the air, and I'd sooner break them off than join them.

"Nan!" Jimmy snaps in a harsh whisper. The waiter is there, ready to slide my plate in front of me, but my elbows are on the table, and I am in the way. I sit back hastily, offering an embarrassed expression.

"I'm sorry. I was lost in thought."

The man smiles at me softly and places the food in front of me. The scent wafts up to my nose and I'm instantly in heaven. It smells delicious and my mouth buds start watering. I glance up at Dominic who isn't even looking at me. He's not only cocky; he's so confident that he doesn't even have to watch me take the first bite to know he is right. I do it quickly, sneaking a spoonful of the soup down before he can see my face. It melts in my mouth like magic, and I'm in pure ecstasy. I hate that he's right, that he knows me like this. And I hate him, for no reason other than he seems to be ahead of the game by two steps every time.

I am three bites in when I look up and see a smug grin on Dominic's face. He hasn't touched his food yet. I enjoy the soup so much I can't even give him a dirty look; it's not physically possible while I'm so enraptured with the food. When I look at Jimmy, however, my heart stops. His face is red, his eyes narrowed. I glance at his hands, fisted next to his plate. He's looking over my shoulder at something or someone behind me. I don't want to know what has Jimmy so worked up, but like every single victim in a thriller, I have to turn to see.

The hair on my arms and the back of my neck stands at attention, tiny little soldiers obeying my fight-or-flight response. I turn slowly, anticipating something that may shock the living hell out of me and I'm not wrong.

Clad in a black tuxedo with silver cummerbund and tie stands my worst nightmare. He grins like a fool with perfect white teeth. His hair is silver now, not the jet-black hair he had when it happened, but it's the same man. Same beady black eyes, same scar on his right eyebrow, same crooked lip. Ronald James Gallagher the third is here?

My chest tightens, my vagina instantly contracts, clamping shut in terror. I think I may throw up, which is a shame because I love this food so much. But the fear response is too strong. My heart is racing and my palms sweaty. I look at Dominic to see him studying me, like a mouse in an incubator being experimented on. In his eyes I see something strange, as if he truly is trying to get a rise out of me or find out what Jimmy and I are made of.

"Good evening, Dominic… Nan, Jimmy," the man says, winking. "Good to see you again." He rests his hands on the back of the empty chair next to me and I feel the bile rising.

Dominic planned this. He had to have. Jimmy is beat-red, ready to explode, and I take his hand. "It's okay, Jimmy. Don't cause a scene."

"A scene?" he snaps in a harsh whisper. "The man tried to kill me."

Dominic's coat flashes again, revealing the gun to both Jimmy and me, and Jimmy calms down like a trained dog. I, however, remain panicked. I'm trembling, unable to stop the adrenaline response in my body. I'm still shaking as Dominic stands, ushering Gallagher away from us, and it doesn't stop until we're back at his place and I'm curled in a ball on the bed.

I don't know what he was trying to prove other than he knows what happened to me, but it ruined me. I take the bottle of whiskey left on the nightstand next to a clean tumbler and drink straight from the source. Before the bottle is halfway gone, I'm passed out, nightmares of Ronald Gallagher clawing at my skin tormenting me.

11

DOMINIC

I sit watching her sleep. She's so peaceful when she's sleeping, which is a far cry from the tantrum she had on the way home and the way she assaulted me with her fists, as if she could hurt me. Her seeing Gallagher was only the tip of the iceberg for what I have planned. She doesn't know, but I'm planning more than just revenge for my mother's death. Nanette brought something to life in me that needed to come to life, a part of me that long lay dead.

Now, she rests, thanks to the tea Mika prepared for her again. She drank it willingly; I didn't even have to sneak it into her without her knowing. Mika told her it would help her sleep, and now she lays on that bed snoring, though her sleep is fitful. I'm sure it's fraught with nightmares, the way she tosses. She moans and lashes out at the air, her brain working out for her in her sleep what she refuses to allow her heart to feel during her waking hours.

I sip my whiskey, wondering what it's like inside her mind. I know how it feels to be trapped in mine. My worst enemies don't suffer the way I do, though I will make them suffer for what they did. There are just a few more pieces left in place, things that need to line up, information I need. Which is where Jimmy comes in. That buffoon better produce the results I need fast, because I need everything to come to fruition at the same time.

I look up as the door opens. It's Jimmy, staggering in with a bloodied nose. He holds a handkerchief to his face to keep the blood from soiling his clothing—my treat after the lashing he suffered. His attempt to rough up Gallagher was unsuccessful again, though this time it was only due to the fact that the bouncer at the restaurant pulled him off the older man. It was a sight and Nanette missed it all. She was already hiding away in my car at the time. Shaken to her core.

"You sick bastard," Jimmy says, bringing the blood-soaked cloth away from his face to look at it then pressing it back there. He sits in one of the leather armchairs in the corner of my room, his eyes fixed on me.

"Sick is a relative term. You don't even know how deep my disease runs, Jimmy." I turn back to the screen where Nanette is displayed, now tossing again. The blanket is wrapped tightly around her torso, her long legs strewn out across the bed. Her black panties peek out, sexy as hell, but not tempting at the moment. I have business, and she needs rest.

Jimmy's trained eyes turn to the monitor, and he gawks. He stands and walks closer to it, leaning in to have a closer look. His jaw drops and he gasps. "That's my sister, you pervert. You're watching my sister? Turn that off!" He reaches for the monitor but there is no off button there. He won't be able to turn it off. His hands frantically search for the button that doesn't exist and his bloody rag falls to the ground, a trickle of the sticky red liquid trailing down his upper lip.

"Save your time, Jimmy. There is no off switch and I'm not turning it off. See how fitful she is? See how tormented she is in her sleep? You did this to her, Jimmy. You."

He turns to glare at me and leans over my desk as if he's forgotten the lesson he just learned. No one messes with Dominic Gusev, at least not those who wish to live.

"You sick bastard. You get off on watching her? Do you watch her change too? Imagine sick fantasies about her and touch yourself?" He pushes the papers off my desk onto the floor and draws the back of his arm across his face, wiping the blood away. It stains his shirt, but that was already ruined during the altercation at the restaurant.

"Who needs to masturbate with Nanette bends over and hikes her skirt freely? She's a nice piece of ass, Jimmy."

My comment has him lurching across my desk fists clenched. He thinks he is stronger than me, but I stop him by grabbing his wrist and twisting it. He rolls off the end of the desk in a heap of whimpers and yelps, until he's nothing more than a pile of sniveling flesh at my feet. I let him go and he scrambles away.

"I can't believe what type of man you are. You are really sick, you know that?"

"Sicker than Gallagher?" I watch him glare at me angrily, narrowing his eyes to thin slits. He's reading me, trying to guess my game, but I have no game. Not this time. I need my answers and my revenge, and Jimmy will have a chance to prove his worth if he just follows my instructions too.

"What do you mean?" He is playing stupid, as if I don't already know that Gallagher molested Nanette for years before raping her right in front of her brother.

"You know what I mean." I rise and straighten my tie, looking back at the monitor. Nanette is moaning, swatting at the air again, her whole body now exposed. The tank top she wears is bunched around her chest; her body now curled into a ball. She's fighting, seeking her own revenge now, and I want to give it to her.

"You know nothing, Dominic. You need to stay out of it. I'm here to do a job for you, nothing more. You keep your hands off my sister." He says his piece from several paces away this time, not trying to harm me. It's a good thing. I don't mess around. Jimmy will be walking out of here much bloodier if he attempts to assault me the way Nanette did in the car. The fight in that woman...

"I know more than you think I do, now I need to know who is after me. Who in my organization wants to take me out and why?" I focus my glare on him, and he cowers in its laser precision. Jimmy isn't a coward like I thought he was, but he hasn't produced the results I need yet.

"I'm working on it. I have it down to a few people who have possible connections, and you just need to give me time." He rubs his wrist where I gripped him and sniffles. The blood sucks back up into his nostril for the moment, but it will come back.

"Names, Jimmy, I need names. I need them before the hit is completed. You realize you don't get paid if I am dead. And you realize that if they kill me, they will know I hired you. It's all over my personal banking. Then what? Then who will protect Nan? Who will avenge her?" I lower my eyes to him again, pursing my lips. He doesn't really realize what's at stake here.

"What?" he stutters, rubbing his nose. He backs into the corner of the room where the leather armchair awaits him. It's darker there, like he's hiding in the shadows afraid of what I'm saying.

"You think you'll just walk away from this if they kill me?" I scoff, laughing at him. "My brothers will hunt you down when this is all said and done. You can't just walk away from this family. You are mine now, Jimmy, like it or not. So, you produce the results I need, or you and your sister are never going to make it out of this alive."

That last part, as true as it may be for him, is never going to be true for Nanette. I've already set a contingency plan in place for her. She will walk away untouched if she is smart. Jimmy, however...

"You can't do that. I was just supposed to get information and take out the mole."

"Things change. Now, get the job done, or you know what happens." I sit down as Jimmy wipes his nose again. He looks terrified now, which is exactly how I want him. "You get this job done, or it's your neck and your sister's too."

"You can't—"

Before he can even reply my pistol is out and I fire off a round above his head. It smashes into the plaster and showers dust across his head and shoulders. He jumps, scared of me, and I shake my head. "You'll never learn, will you? Get out of my office."

Jimmy jumps up and rushes out and I hear the front door slam. I glance at the monitor. Nanette doesn't even stir. She lays there peaceful now, the night terrors gone for the moment, and I reach behind me to my old liquor cabinet and pour myself another glass of whiskey. I need to think, need time to process the anger coursing through me.

If Nanette was awake, I'd dump it into her, make her feel how powerful I am, that I can do things she only dreams of. But she needs rest, and I need revenge.

I wander out into the hallway, finding my way to my mother's old room. The door is locked. I use the key hidden in my pocket to unlock it and let myself in. I'm so close to finding out who did this, who let that maniac into this house to hurt her. Who plans to murder me too, to silence me so I won't let the public know what a monster they have creeping around them.

I walk up to the large portrait of her and stare at it, feeling rage thrumming through my veins. I've cried too many tears over this painting and stared at it for too many hours. No child should have to go through what I went through, and I'm not talking about the savage way the man almost gutted me. I'm talking about the way I walked in on him raping her, forcing himself inside of her while he covered her mouth with his hand.

Fury leaps up in my chest and I down the whiskey, throwing the glass against the wall in a huff. It smashes on the wall, remnants of whiskey and glass shards scattering to the ground beneath where it hits. My chest heaves with unspent emotion. I can't think straight. Pictures flash through my head—Mom on the ground, the man assaulting her. I try for the millionth time to imagine the man's face, to remember what I've blocked out for so long, but it's no use. His face is a blur, and my memory is foggy.

"Ahhhhh!" I scream out, letting the anger take hold of me. I won't hold back anymore. It's killing me. I lash out, smashing first the lamp then the vase on the dresser. I lose control, destroying the room the way Nanette destroyed her room. Nothing is left untouched, nothing that is, except my mother's portrait.

When the room is trashed and I am spent, leaning over with my hands on my knees, I look up into her eyes. She haunts me, begging me to find the man who hurt her and make him pay. Her gaze pleads with me; it has since the day I tried to stop him. I wound up in an ambulance bleeding out, gasping for air. The scar across my chest and side are proof of the justice that is due. And that man will pay.

He will pay for hurting her. He will pay for hurting me. For the days I wasn't allowed to even enter this room. For the hours I cried at her door, asking her to let me come in—once I'd returned from the hospital. For the way my father changed—the darkness that still clouds his eyes to this day as he prepares to hand the family over to me. The man responsible for destroying my family will not go unpunished.

I straighten and see blood on my hands, likely from something I broke. I rub it on my slacks and feel the key still in my pocket. This room is sacred. No one comes in here but me. I don't have energy to clean tonight, so I leave it, letting myself out of the room and locking up behind me. I never had to lock up until Nanette came to stay. Now I have to force myself to remember.

My hand shakes as I put the key in the lock, jingling against the door-knob. I need to relax, to sit and let my blood pressure come down. What I need is release, the kind only sex gives me, but Nanette is sleeping, and I can't even think of another woman right now. Nan and I have too much, we're too similar.

It's dark as I slink back into my office, hiding away behind my desk. Mika has shut off the lights, probably assuming I've retired for the night. But the closed-circuit TV still plays in Nanette's room. She's covered now, likely woke up to a chill and realized she had tossed her blanket in her restless sleep. She's peaceful again, as if the night torments haven't even affected her this evening at all.

She's beautiful as she lays there, angelic even. She reminds me of my mother too, a tortured soul in her own right. I can't let that happen to Nanette, what happened to my mom. My fists clench instinctively, and I feel protective. She is mine now, whether she likes it or not, and I protect my things. No one will touch her, and no one will harm her, not if I have anything to say about it.

And the sleazy way Gallagher looked at her, as if he'd tasted forbidden fruit, I could have slit his throat right there, but that pound of flesh is not mine to take. All I can do is make sure Nanette does not fall to the same fate that Mom did.

She stirs, tossing the covers off again, and I see her silken form stretched across the bed. Her hand trails to her mound, massaging it in her sleep. I wonder if she does this often, touching herself because of a dream. It arouses me to watch, though I can't help but also wonder if she is thinking of me, or of someone else. Nanette has led a very colorful life since her time with Gallagher. I want to end that for her. She doesn't need to give her body away to abusive rich men. Not when she has everything, she needs to be free of it forever—that compulsion to replay that event over and over in ways that make her feel powerful instead of powerless.

She doesn't even see how she does it, but I do. I see how she uses her feminine wiles to try to twist my emotions, make herself feel like the seductress rather than the dominated. She tries to get back at Gallagher in her own way, but it will never work, and when she realizes this, blood will flow. I just pray it isn't hers.

12

NANETTE

I awake with a start to an empty room. I'm tired, too tired. I feel like the drug Mika put in my tea last night was too strong, but I accepted it with gladness. After what happened at the restaurant, I knew I would struggle to sleep, and I was right. I feel like I've been through the wars, body aches, headache, and grogginess.

I climb out of bed and dress in some shorts and a t-shirt. I don't want to stay locked in this room all day. Dominic may have purposely triggered something horrible just to prove a point, but I'm not a victim. I refuse to allow him to control me like that. I am powerful, strong enough to push past what happened to me years ago, so why not this too?

My feet slide into the ballet flats, and I am out the door, headed toward the scent of bacon and eggs. Mika is ready for me as soon as I walk in, as if she is watching me sleep so she knows when to start my meal. I wonder how she does this, and if she does it for Dominic too, or if I'm special. I slouch on the seat and she slides breakfast in front of my eager eyes.

"Don't eat too quickly," she said, studying my face. "You look pale."

I feel a bit off too, but I don't tell her that. I use the fork to carefully cut a bite of egg, my mouth watering, but the moment it is on my tongue, I feel nauseous. The flavors seem off, as if my tastebuds are lying to me. Part of me fears that Dominic drugged the eggs too, but why? What reason would he have to drug me more? I've already slept off the worst of it.

"Not hungry?" Mika wipes her hands on a towel and watches me. I try another bite with the same effect.

"I'm sorry, it tastes off. I'm starving, but I just think I'll pass." I push the plate away, my stomach growling in protest. I can't eat food I don't trust. Maybe there is nothing wrong with it, but knowing Dominic adds sleeping medicine to my tea doesn't give me much confidence when it comes to the food now.

"Suit yourself." Mika picks up the plate and dumps it in the trash. "Dominic is out for a while. You can visit the library or sit in the garden, though if you're going out you should do it soon. It looks like it'll rain." Her eyes shift toward the window, and I follow her gaze. Storm clouds hang over the property like the ones that haunt me in my dreams.

"Thanks, I'll go to the library."

I stand and walk out of the kitchen, this time careful to avoid the sacred room that earned me the "punishment" last time. I want Dominic to come for me like he did last time, though. The way he thought he punished me, only to leave me pleading for more of him like an addict. The man is cocaine in a suit, addictive and dangerous, but the only thing that sates my need for control. And after last night, I need my control back.

I take a deep breath and stride towards the windows in the corner, flipping on the lights.

The room is illuminated with an array of books—more than I have ever seen before. Each one contains tales of adventure that I can only dream of having. He has so many books, there's no way he could read them all—but I hope that given enough time, I will be able to. Reading has always been my sanctuary; it allows me to leave this world behind and find solace in some foreign land. A place where I don't fear for my life: where I can explore whatever my heart desires without ever leaving the comfort of home.

I walk the length of the room, drawing my finger along one row of books. There isn't a speck of dust, a testament to Mika's housekeeping. She runs a tight ship, and I suspect she may be ex-military. Each one is cataloged too, like in a real library. I see an old-fashioned card catalog, probably a remnant taken from a city library as they went digital. Its tiny drawers are labeled with Dewey Decimal identification. I fumble through a few cards in the top right drawer, seeing nothing that piques my interest, so I head for the ladder. It is stuck in place, and it takes me a while to move it, but once I get it going, it glides along the wall with ease.

There is a particular book on the second shelf from the top that I see. It intrigues me with its red leather-bound cover. I climb the ladder and precariously reach for it. I'm not quite close enough, but my fingers stretch out to grasp it. As I pull it back to my chest, I see the title says, "Anne of Green Gables," and it brings back fond memories of childhood. I descend the ladder with my prize and look around the room.

There are two couches facing each other on opposite sides of an old wooden coffee table. All of them are Victorian Era pieces, preserved with impeccable taste. But I choose the floral wingback chair in the corner next to the Tiffany lamp. It looks comfortable and it draws me in. I sit in the chair with my grumbling stomach and open to the first page.

In a matter of moments, the story captivates me, and I'm drawn in. I sit for hours reading the story, ignoring my bladder and my thirst. I'm more than halfway through when Mika finds me, as if she wears an alert bracelet tied to my hydration levels. She sets a cup of cool lemonade next to me along with a few tiny finger sandwiches and smiles.

"My favorite too," she whispers, a twinkle in her eye, and when she leaves, my eyes follow her. I set the book down as I sip the lemonade, and I notice a basket by the door which I had previously passed by. I was in awe of the books; I never saw the basket containing old newspapers. It has me curious, so I pick up one of the finger sandwiches and stand, walking over to the old newspapers.

In it I find some newer papers with more recent headlines. Things that happened within the past few months. When I dig deeper, I see things that happened years ago, clippings of the war in Iraq, things that happened in Russia in the eighties. But my heart stops when I read the headline on one particular paper.

"Young Man Barely Survives Vicious Robbery Attempt."

Jimmy's face is plastered on the paper's front page, details of the horror he suffered revealed in the story's columns. My heart races. Dominic knows everything, not just what happened to me. And he knew this before he hired Jimmy; I am willing to bet on it. Maybe this is why he hired Jimmy too, to gain some leverage over him, and when it didn't work, he took me. Dominic has been snooping too much and it infuriates me. What right does he have to do all this research on us? Play us like we are some cheap violins or something? And yet he remains so secretive to me...

Anger drives me, motivating me to do what I'm about to do. He hated when I was in that room with the painting, and I never did remember where I've seen that woman before. So, it's the first place I go. I march down the hall, shoving that finger sandwich in my mouth, and try the knob. It's locked, which frustrates me. He really doesn't want me in here, and now I have to go in. It's a matter of principle now. He snoops around my past; I snoop around his past.

With no way to pick a lock, I race up to my room to rifle through things until I find a bobby pin in the bathroom. It's exactly what I need to pick the lock, so I stuff it in my pocket and hurry back down to the door, checking on my way several times to make sure no one is watching. The knob is old, the type that uses a skeleton key, not a modern lock. While I've had my share of locks to pick, this one challenges me. I work at it for several minutes before I give up.

In frustration, determined to find out what Dominic is hiding, I look around the hallway for anything that may help me gain entrance to this damn room. My eyes land on a large metal bust of some man I don't recognize. It will do the trick.

I heft the bust over to the door and hoist it as high as my arms will allow. It's heavy, so gravity does most of the work as I bring it down with force on the doorknob. It only takes one hit, and the knob breaks free, bouncing a few times before rolling along the hallway floor. The bust drops to my feet and I leap up to avoid it smashing my feet. It, too, goes rolling, but stops much more quickly due to its odd shape. At least the bust doesn't break, which is more than I can say for the door. Even the wood has a crack that runs from the knob to the striker plate, and the door swings open easily.

I stand there a bit chuffed with myself for breaking in, but then I waste no time marching into the room. It isn't at all how I saw it last. It looks more like my room after I smashed everything. Drawers are turned out, lamps smashed. The only thing in this room left intact is the painting on the wall and the four-post bed, though the sheets are torn from it as well. I stand in the doorway for a moment surveying the damage and all I can see is pain—Dominic's pain.

"I'm going to find out who you are, Dominic, and then I'm going to ruin you." I head into the chaos, sorting through papers and other things laying around. Part of me hesitates, like I'm intruding on something I have no business knowing. But I'm so angry with him, so enraged that he thinks he can manipulate me and my brother. I have to do this. I will myself to move into the room farther, uncovering things carefully so I don't do any more damage than what is already done.

Clothing is strewn about, women's clothing. It isn't modern clothing though, almost as if this room were a time capsule, commemorating something that happened twenty years ago when fashion was very different than today. I recognize one piece of clothing on the ground and pick it up, holding it in the air. It is the same outfit as the one in the portrait on the wall. This room belonged to this woman. I know it.

Mesmerized for a moment, staring at the portrait, I drop the dress and continue my search. Glass shards pepper the scattered clothing and papers. I'm careful not to step on any more of them than is necessary to sort through things. A piece of glass crunches beneath my foot and I look down. The corner of a brown binder peeks out at me, and I kneel to uncover it. It's buried beneath the pink bedding that was once on the bed.

I pull the binder out to see it isn't a binder at all. It's an old family picture album. The cover has a picture of Dominic when he was a child, hair parted down the center. He's adorable, as if time is what soiled him and ruined his personality. I fold open the front cover and look through the pages, relaxing back until I'm seated and leaning against the bed. The images tell a fascinating tale of five brothers.

I flip through the entire photo album but all I see are pictures of boys being boys—a few images of cars and one of an old house, maybe this house before it was updated. So, I pick up another album unearthed when I pulled this one out. This one has no image on the front cover, so I'm left to my imagination as I fold open the cover. The first picture is of a couple on their wedding day. The woman is the same from the portrait on the wall. She is happy, wearing a white dress; they stand cutting their cake.

It looks like a happy union, smiling faces in every single one of the pictures in the album. But the more pages I turn, the glummer the woman looks. Her smiles fade to calm expressions, then to sadness that hides in her eyes. Something happened to her, something that hurt her desperately. Something maybe she didn't speak about.

I look up at the portrait, clearly painted before this horrible event, and I wonder what it was that hurt her to steal the life from her eyes. My heart clenches in my chest as I recall my own life-altering event and wonder if hers was similar. I find myself connecting with her somehow, though I don't know who she is still. My anger with Dominic has faded for the moment as my curiosity about this woman takes over. I look back down at the album, with only a few more pages left to turn.

My breath catches as I turn the page and see the next photo. This one isn't a picture at all, but a newspaper clipping. Her eyes claw at my skin, haunting me, threatening me now with violence because I know who she is. I know what happened to her. And I know where it happened. I feel dizzy, like I'll pass out, but my body leaps into action. I bolt off the ground and stand there, letting the album drop to my feet.

"Holy fuck," I mutter, backing away. I shouldn't be here, not here, not in this room. Not when he is… "Oh god," I mumble, still backing away. This place, it's where she was attacked, and I am crossing lines I never knew existed.

Fear pushes me to leave, to head out the front door and run away. I know exactly where I am now, but if I leave, he'll only come after me. He's already proven how much he knows, and now I know how deadly he is, what his name is, why he keeps it a secret. The Gusev's are organized crime—Bratva—and Dominic is far more dangerous than Jimmy knows. How on earth could he get into bed with these guys?

I stumble down the hallway to the stairs. Mika passes me on my way up; she's heading down. "I was looking for you. How were your sandwiches? You finished the book?" she asks, but I pass like a ghost in the night. "Are you okay?" she pries, but I can't even look at her. Does she know who he is? Is she a captive too?

I mutter something unintelligible and walk straight to my room and lock the door, as if that puny lock will stop him. When he sees what

I've done, the broken knob, the room—the albums. Fuck, I forgot to put them back. God, I'm in trouble. He will be furious. He will hurt me. He will punish me and this time it won't be sex. He will kill me. His identity is exposed and there is nothing I can do about it. Knowing what I know will not save me—it's a death warrant.

I curl up on the bed and cover myself, trying to hide from the terror seeping into my pores. This is worse than seeing Gallagher again, worse than me fearing Jimmy dies. I'm shaking so bad I may throw up. I want to go home. I want Jimmy.

13

DOMINIC

Another anger-fueled meeting with Nick and Leo, and I'm ready for a drink. The arms shipment fell through, and now I'm upside down on that deal. It's nothing I can't fix, but it does raise suspicions when it comes to those two. I've been watching everyone more closely since I discovered the plot against my life, including those two; I just wish Jimmy would bring me something conclusive.

As I drive home, I reflect on the family. Sven, my younger brother by only a few years, has been distant, trouble with a lady friend I assume. I don't think for a second that he's involved. He has no interest in running the family—he's stated that a number of times. I believe him too. It's a big job and it carries as much stress as it does weight and prestige. Not many people are willing to put their life on the line for something like this, not to mention their name and reputation.

A name like Gusev is synonymous with power, which is likely why someone is trying to get rid of me. And it makes sense how someone from within may want to shift Sven to the top. After all, a man who does not want to lead is easily swayed by voices within to do as they please. His authority means nothing to him. My father knows this too, which is why I am the obvious choice, because I seek the position with the interest of leading the family into the next generation of business. Not just because I'm the oldest son.

I turn down my street. The overcast sky paints a glum gray over the houses on the street. Mine sits at the far end of a cul-de-sac, down a narrow lane past the security gate. Scarsdale is home; it always has been even long after Father moved away from this place to a penthouse in the city. I could never leave. This place, where Mom died, holds too many memories. I have a fondness for the old trees that reach their branches out to shade the home's eaves, and the bushes that grow out front used to be my playground. All four of my brothers used to play in them, pretending they were our castles or ships, whether we were on land or at sea.

I park near the front door and make my way up the steps. It's been a long afternoon, and I'm ready for a drink. I'm expecting a call from Jimmy later this evening again, but I doubt he's gotten any more information. The man moves slower than a snail. He's thorough though, so despite my anger over how long he's taking, at least I know I hired the right man for the job. I give him a hard time, but he is truly the best. If this works out and he wants a place in my organization, I know I can trust him too. That is a rare commodity in this business.

As I let myself in, I instantly know something is wrong. The house is quiet like normal, but there is a scent in the air I can't place. It's sweet, but not from Mika's baking or Nanette's perfume. And it doesn't smell like the flowers from the garden. The low pressure has all scents outdoors dampened as a storm front approaches. This smell inside the house is almost sinister, as if ghosts are reaching up from the grave to taunt me, and I'm drawn away from my office to my mother's room, where I rarely go—until Nanette drew my attention back to it.

I walk quietly to the hallway and before I am ten paces in, I notice the door is open. The doorknob rests on the floor on the opposite side of the hall, the bust of my Uncle Herbert on the floor next to pieces of a splintered door. My first instinct is to draw my weapon. Someone has violated my privacy, broken my door open. I move forward in stealth, pointing the gun in the room as I nudge it open with my toe.

It's still a disaster, almost exactly how I left it when I trashed it, but not quite. I see things have been moved, the blankets, a few items of clothing. I tore the sheets off the bed last; the clothing should not be on top of it. And who would want anything to do with this old room? There is nothing of value in here, except an old portrait of a dead woman.

The farther I get into the room, the more I see amiss. Yes, I see it, even though it was destroyed when I left. I can see how things are not how they should be. Papers are moved, dresser drawers up righted. But what catches my eye the most are the family albums. I holster my weapon, assured there has not been a real intruder, as my chest begins to tighten. Nanette has been in here again, snooping.

I stoop next to the albums that lay open with images of my childhood staring back at me. She's gone through my things, searching for God only knows what. Her prying eyes and fingers have touched every- thing in here after I specifically told her to stay out and locked the door. She didn't even stealthily pick the lock; she broke the damn knob right off and barged in. And why didn't Mika stop her?

Infuriated, I stand and clench my fingers into fists, then storm out of the room and directly up the steps to her room. The door is shut as I approach. The sight makes my blood boil, but not as much as when I reach out to jiggle the knob only to find it locked. I'm so enraged, I plant the heel of my foot just above the knob, breaking the door open. The doorjamb splinters as the door slams open and bounce on the wall, swinging back at me with force. I stop it with a hand and glare at her.

Nanette lays on the bed curled in a ball shaking. Her scared eyes peek out from beneath the corner of the red fabric. I can see how terrified she is, and she should be. She broke my rules and now she will suffer the consequences.

"What the hell were you thinking?" I ask her, charging over to the bed. I grab the corner of the blanket and pull it hard, uncovering her in one movement. She grasps out as if trying to stop me from exposing her, but I move too quickly, stealing her covers. I expect her to back away, cower before me against the wooden headboard, but she surprises me.

Nanette leaps off the bed like a feral cat, swinging and clawing at me. Her assault isn't just physical; she screams and sobs, slamming her hands into my chest. When I grab both her wrists and she cannot move, she spits in my face. I push her backward onto the bed where she bounces and finally does what I thought she would do first. She scurries away like a scared little mouse.

"You went in my room again!" I move closer, grabbing her foot and pulling her back toward me. "You knew I told you not to do that. I gave you orders to stay out of there. I locked the fucking door."

"You're a monster," she hisses, yanking her leg out of my grasp.

"My property is destroyed. The door busted in... What were you thinking?"

"You're hiding something," she snaps, evading my grasp as she rolls off the opposite side of the bed. With the mattress between us we are at a standoff.

"I'm hiding something?" I move to one end, and she walks the other way. She'll be over the bed and out the door before I can catch her, so I move back. When she centers herself, the real death stare ensues.

"You've been snooping into me and Jimmy. I saw the newspapers in the library." She runs a shaking hand through her hair and all I can think about is teaching her a lesson. It isn't nice to pry.

"Yes, because he's doing a job for me. I need to know everything. You have no right snooping in my home." I loosen my tie, feeling my blood pressure rise. "Now I need to teach you what happens when you break my rules, and dammit, Nanette, I never wanted this to happen."

She backs away and it's my opening. As she bumps into the night stand, I dart across the bed, snatching both of her wrists into one hand. "You should mind your own business, Nanette. Bad girls get punished, and you're going to get it now." I turn her around, wrapping both my arms around her and pinning her against my body. It doesn't please me to have to threaten her, and I know nothing I can do to her is really punishment; she likes it too much. But she has to know I'm serious, even if that is only scaring her a little.

I bend her over the bed and pin her down with one hand as I undo my belt, making sure she hears it as it slides out of my belt loops. I fully intend to fuck her—dump this anger and frustration in an orgasmic release, but not until she understands how she wronged me. She can't just go through my things.

She winces as the belt buckle jingles and whimpers. "I know who you are." Her voice is shaking, but she does not hold back. She's not timid at all as she says it, which makes me freeze, belt in hand, ready to whip her. "I know who you are, and I can ruin you."

I remove my hand from her back, shocked at her admission. It isn't at all what I expected her to say.

"You what?"

She straightens and turns to face me, inches from my body. Her tits brush over my arm and make my skin tingle. She may know my name, but she has no clue who she's dealing with. I stare her down, daring her to do her worst as I lower my arm and wait for her to speak again.

"I had this 'date' one night. His name was Victor Horatio. I know it was probably a fake name, but he knew shit." She is bold now, leaning against me, posturing. Not even my own brothers would do this, stand up to me like this. This woman has guts. She glares at me, raising her chin to continue. "He told me about you, Dominic Gusev. Told me you were Bratva, the leader or some shit. He told me your mother slit her own throat just to make you the man you are today."

The instant the words leave her mouth, my hand leaves my side. It's instinct. I don't mean to hurt her, but she yelps and sits on the edge of the bed holding her cheek. Fury burns inside my veins, and I take a step back.

"Don't you ever speak of my mother that way again," I hiss. I can't stay here, or I will hurt her. There will not be any angry sex to sate my lust and teach her a lesson. It will be dangerous for her. So, I storm out, slamming the door behind me but it bounces open. It won't even shut now. There is no way to restrain her and keep her there, and she is on my heels like a yappy dog, barking while it chases me down to my office.

"You admit it then? You're the son of the pakhan? You're going to lead the largest organized crime family in this city?"

Nanette's bare feet slap on the marble as she chases after me. I can't stand the sound. It unnerves me, brings back horrible memories of that sound, the skin slapping skin. I need to drown it. I go directly to my liquor cabinet, and I skip the glass, downing several gulps of my best Scotch while she pries more.

"You're watching me? That's my room!" she snaps, pointing at the closed-circuit TV. "That's insane. You're a pervert. How can you do that!" Her fists pummel me again while I down another shot. No one does this to me—no one. So why do I let her? What is she to me that I don't defend myself?

"Stop!" I snap, blocking her from hitting my chest as I set the bottle down, but she does not stop swinging. "I said, stop, Nanette!"

I grab her wrists and back her up to the wall, pinning her there as I catch my breath. She squirms, breaking her hands free from my grasp and darts away. I whip around to see her pick up the small television and fling across the room in my direction. I dodge it and it smashes on the wall. I watch it shatter and as I turn to see where she is next, I see the bottle of Scotch flying at me. She continues to throw things that I have to dodge, until I wrap my arm around her waist and pick her up, hauling her away from the desk so she can't reach anything else.

"You sick bastard. You're toying with us! What kind of sick game are you playing?" Her tantrum continues, clawing at my arm, kicking me, but inside I know she is tiring. So, I hold her there, letting her wear herself out as the whiskey kicks in. It tingles my chest then relaxes me as she screams, and when she is spent, heaving and sobbing, I wrap my other arm around her waist and whisper in her ear.

"I'm not at all who you think I am, and if you let me, the monster can be your friend."

"What do you think this is? Beauty and the Beast?" She scratches my arm again, and I spin her around to face me.

"I could have killed your brother that day, Nanette. When he didn't have what I wanted, and he demanded to back out. I could have put that bullet into his head instead of the wall. You are the reason I didn't." She stills and looks up into my eyes. There is hatred there, but also lust. She is nearer to the center of power than she's ever been, and I can see the desire in her eyes to conquer it, dominate me, manipulate me into revealing myself, but she's already seen it—the beast in all its fury.

"The scar on your chest... Was it him?" she asks, voice shaking. She won't look away, and I won't respond. Instead, I kiss her, because it's what she really wants, and because now that she's seen me, there is no going back.

14

NANETTE

H is kiss takes my breath away. It isn't a kiss of anger; it's different. It's hungry and needy, not demanding. I kiss him back because I need to; I need release. I'm furious with him, terrified of who he really is, but this is my toxic trait. I have to take what he's stolen from me, the power, the knowing. He won't answer my question about the scar on his chest, but my gut tells me he got it trying to defend his mother, and now he wants revenge on the man who did it.

I want revenge too, the type that makes Gallagher drop to his knees and beg for mercy, the way I begged for mercy, the way Jimmy begged for mercy. But I'll never even get justice, let alone revenge. Not with Gallagher. But men like Dominic are easier. Sex is their weakness, the way I conquer them and take my power back. They are all the same, chasing pussy and showing how vulnerable they are, and I give them what they want and when I'm done, I know I have the power to do that to them. All while making myself feel good too.

"God, you infuriate me," I tell him as I tear at his shirt. His greedy hands pull at my clothing too, tugging my shorts until they tear at the waistband and slide down to my knees.

He's greedy now, hands searching me as his lips devour mine. When his fingers touch my skin, it sends electric jolts through me. He presses his whole body against mine, grinding his erect cock against my belly and I shiver in response. He greedily thrusts himself against me, reaching under my shirt to slide his hands over my stomach then up to my tits. The sudden touch of his skin leaves me breathless, my heart pounding in my ears; I struggle to take deep breaths. My head is too full of faraway thoughts and lust-driven urges to breathe properly, which suits him fine because he just grinds himself against me and kisses me deeper.

I'm about to explode with passion. The way he's pulling at my clothes sends tingling sensations throughout my skin, his strong hands pressing against my bare back. It makes me feel dizzy, trapped in this whirlwind of hunger and lust. His kiss turns even more forceful as I feel him unbuttoning his pants with a swift motion. My hands, too, are unable to stay still. I'm tugging at his pants, until they give way and fall in a pool of fabric around his ankles.

"Touch me," he demands into my mouth. I grab hold of his girth and stroke it before lowering my mouth to tease the swollen head with my tongue. "I know you love this" he whispers as he pulls me tighter against him. I can feel his cock, deliciously huge and hard inside my throat. I move against it shamelessly, feeling him shudder as I use my whole mouth to glide over him.

When I glance up at him, his eyes are closed, and his mouth is slightly parted. I run the tip of my tongue up and down the length of him before swirling my tongue over his swollen head. I can feel his cock twitch wildly in my grip. "I love the way you feel inside my mouth," I admit openly before taking him into my throat again. I nip at the head of his dick, and he grunts.

"Fuck," he moans. I do it again, unbelievably excited by the way he's sounding so turned on.

I moan in response, feeling my own need building between my legs. I will bring him to the edge, then withhold, because I need this power over him. It fixes something inside me when I do this, makes me feel strong. Gallagher took that power from me years ago and I've been doing this ever since, just to stay sane.

I feel his hands tangle down through my hair and come to a rest at the base of my neck as I use my lips to pleasure him. I can't describe the wickedness that comes over me when I look up at him and see the pleasure cross his face. With one hand under my chin, I hold him still while I move my mouth over his throbbing cock, letting its huge size push into the very back of my throat. His head slumps backward as he throws his hand up to fist his hair, moaning out in ecstasy.

"Fuck," he groans weakly before placing both his hands on either side of my head. He pushes me against himself again and again, so hard I can barely breathe. The air escapes from my lungs as I shudder from shock and pleasure, struggling to work with this building sensation.

I cradle his balls, feeling them drawing up. He's close, and I'm not letting him finish, not like this. But before I can even pull away on my own, Dominic grabs a fistful of my hair and yanks me back. "Not like that," he hisses, forcing me to stand.

"How then?" I smirk, watching him out of the corner of my eye. My head cranes at an odd angle until he lets me go with a growl of desire. He pushes me backward until my ass rests against the desk, then sweeps an arm across it, clearing it for our fuck session.

I try to lift my hips up to sit on the edge, but he's faster than me, picking me up and placing me there. He tugs my jeans off, then rips my panties. He must have a thing for torn panties because this is becoming a habit. I spread my legs to him, and he doesn't hesitate to slide his cock right into me.

"Fuck, you're so wet," he grunts as he pushes himself into me. He grabs hold of my legs and pulls them until he's deep between my thighs. I throw my own arms around his neck and dig my nails into his back as he thrusts hard inside me again, then again and a third time.

"I love fucking you," he grunts in my ear. "I love all the ways I can fuck you, the way you look at me while I'm filling you with cock. I love the way you feel around me, the way you don't stop until I'm soaked with cum. You're the best fucking sex I've ever had."

I run my tongue over his chin and bite at his lip before kissing him soft and sweet. If there's one thing that makes me come harder than anything else, it's when I know I've got the power, and I know I do right now.

"Girls like you need to be fucked hard," he insists pitilessly as he thrusts himself inside me. I gasp and dig my nails into his back, with nothing else left to hold on to.

It's deeper than any other time we've been together, more desperate and out of control. His hands slide up to grip my shoulders, my pussy clenching around him and releasing everything I need to give. The pleasure crawls through every inch of my body, while without warning; sweat starts dripping off of every available surface in my body as he works me over.

"Fuck me," I yell at him as I let my head drop back and shudder around him. His cock is throbbing hard and fast, pounding into me so hard that he's knocking the desk against the wall, shaking the framed picture with every thrust.

His hands grip my thighs so tightly I know he will leave bruises, but I'm close. My body is tensing, my pussy clamping down around him, and then he pulls out. In a split second, he grabs my hair again, forcing my face downward as he strokes his cock. He explodes, cum spraying on my nose, cheeks and chin. The startling lack of dick inside of me makes me whimper, my mouth dropping open, and his cum squirts inside of my mouth. The salty, chunky liquid makes me nearly gag, and I yelp.

"What the fuck!" I shout, coughing. I try to push him away, but he's too strong. He smacks my ass hard, and I shudder as I feel his warm cum drip down my throat and all over my neck.

"Bad girls don't get to come, Nanette," Dominic says as he looks me up and down unhurriedly. The bastard is entirely too smug for what he just did. He lets go of my hair and I straighten, the need between my legs still throbbing.

I lick my lips with that last taste still bitter in my mouth as my body slides off the edge of the desk to the floor where I sit feeling shocked. He can't do this to me. I'm supposed to be the one with power. I need this; I need release. My pussy hurts so bad I almost cry.

"You sick bastard," I shout, pushing myself up off the floor. As I do I pick up his stapler, tossed to the floor as he cleared his desk. I throw it at him, and he dodges it, then yanks his pants up.

"You were told not to go in that room." His gravelly growl infuriates me. I frantically look around the room for something else to throw at him, but he is there, scooping me up. He tosses me over his shoulder fireman style, and I pummel his back with my fists.

"Put me down!" I shout, kicking and flailing. He carries me out the door of his office and down the hallway. We head up the stairs, passing my room with its broken door. He ducks into a different room; all the while, I'm still pounding his back. When he tosses me onto a bed, a squeak escapes my lips as I bounce. "You jerk!" I am sobbing now, shaking with rage. He can't do this to me.

This room has no clothing, no pleasant bed spread. There is no window, no vase of flowers. It's plain, as if it has been ignored since his mother died, since his family left. I curl into a ball and scoot back against the headboard. My sobs come harder. I feel powerless, exposed, vulnerable. I feel weak. Too weak, and he is the reason.

"I hate you!"

"Hate is such a strong word, Nan." Dominic stands there staring at me smugly as he unbuttons the cuffs of his long-sleeve button down and rolls them up. His shirt still hangs open, the scar on his chest exposed. He catches me looking at it through my tears. I'm supposed to be the one with power right now, not him, not this.

"Well it's true. I hate you." It's not true, not even a little. I'm scared of him, yes, but I don't hate him. How can I hate him? How, when I know he knows what happened to me, and he still wanted me enough to fuck me? He knows and he thinks of me like he thinks of his mother, a victim that needs rescued. Only, I don't want to be the victim; I want to be the powerful one. He raped me of that power. Why? To prove something to me?

"We have too much in common for you to hate me. You know that." He moves closer, pushing the sleeves up a bit farther. I wipe at my eyes, still furious that he withheld an orgasm from me. My body throbs, moisture still dripping out of me as I realize my face is covered in his sticky release. I touch it gingerly, disgusted by the tack texture. He tosses his handkerchief at me and I wipe myself clean, then blow my nose.

"You don't know me," I tell him, throwing the soiled rag onto the floor.

"I know you, Nan. I know you better than you know yourself." He moves closer, turning the bed down on one side. "Lie down," he orders, and I want to protest, but a part of me still wants that orgasm. So, I slide beneath the covers, letting my fingers slip into the soft folds between my legs.

When he climbs into bed, I expect him to touch me, to say dirty things, but he doesn't. He forces me to face away from him. Then he pulls me against his chest. I hate this, this vulnerability. I don't want to be held. I want fucked. I squirm uncomfortably, feeling tears welling up again. He doesn't know me. If he knew me, he would just make me come again. I whimper, ready to protest, to beg him to make me come. I know that makes me the weak one, but my body needs release now.

"I know you Nanette," he coos, squeezing me more tightly. "This is what you need right now."

I want to fight, to resist him, but tears well up. "I don't need held. I need release."

"You need to understand vulnerability and what it's like to feel safe again." His words prick my heart, and the tears spring from my eyes. I don't want to learn this. I was vulnerable once, trusting even. Gallagher ruined that; he stole from me. I can still feel the sensation of his hands touching me, his body moving against mine.

I can still see the look of shock on Jimmy's face as he was forced to watch it in horror. He protested, begged, but Gallagher was evil, and I was weak. I swore I would never be weak again. So, I wrestle against Dominic's arms, pushing at him, clawing at him. A scream erupts from my throat, a scream I've suppressed for more than ten years. I jerk my body, trying to get away, but his arms tighten down around me. I can't move.

"Fuck you!" I scream, drawing blood on his arms. "Fuck you and fuck your business." I am sobbing, flailing to get away from him but he is too strong.

"I saw too, Nanette. I saw what happened to my mother. Tried to defend her. You're right," he says in a low tone, so low I almost miss what he says next. "The scar is from him, the man who hurt her. He nearly cut me in two when I attacked him trying to get him off her."

I can't fight anymore. My strength is spent. I go limp in his arms, sobbing. It's an eerie, haunting cry straight out of my gut. Dominic's grip doesn't go slack though, and for that I'm grateful. He holds me more tightly as he speaks quietly to me.

"They hurt her and I'm going to get revenge for that." He kisses the back of my head and I wince. It's too much, too similar to Gallagher.

"Jimmy and me, we're not that different, you know? I'm using him to help me get revenge, and then I will take care of him. You'll see, Nan. You'll be free of this, and you'll never have to do this again."

I don't know what he means by "take care of him" but it terrifies me. When men like Dominic say they will take care of something it is bad, very bad.

"My mother's attacker will pay dearly, and the mole within my organization will go down. I'll be rid of that problem and then Jimmy will get what's coming to him."

I stiffen as he says the words, my gut still churning. A mix of strong emotions has me on a yoyo. I want to hate him, lash out and scream, but part of me feels strangely comforted here in spite of feeling powerless. Dominic has the power now, and for the first time in my life, I'm not entirely traumatized by that. That someone else has power over me. Somehow, I trust that he won't use that power to hurt me. He sees my game, using sex as a way to feel strong and brave, and he refuses to let me stoop to that level. But he could kill my brother, so why am I okay with lying in his arms crying? Why do I let him make me weak?

15

DOMINIC

I stir somewhere around one a.m., curled up around Nanette. She snores lightly, at peace after hours of crying and fighting me. I hated tearing her down, exposing her, but the only way to build correctly is to start with a clear foundation. Nanette has played games her whole life, so much so that she has no clue who she is. I see her. I know her game because I play it too, and I hate that she has to hide.

My phone buzzes in my pocket, revealing the reason I stirred awake. Without shaking the bed too much, I reach for my phone and see it's Red. He sent a text telling me to call him urgently, and when he says urgently, I know what that means. He has news, or he's been threatened. I hope it's the former, because if someone threatens my family they threaten me, and I just can't be bothered with killing people right now. I have bigger fish to fry.

Slowly, I extract myself from the bed, careful not to wake her. For a moment I watch her sleep. The dim light streaming in from the adjoining bathroom is just enough to see her peaceful expression. When this is all over, I will make sure she never has to fall asleep in torment the way she did tonight. She deserves nothing less than what my mother deserved, and if I can stop her from the same fate, I will.

I walk out into the hallway, bringing my phone to my ear with Red's number ringing through. I head down the stairs to my office, tucking my shirt in as I go. It's likely Red has something substantial, otherwise why would he message me in the middle of the night? So, I head for my keys and my wallet, both on the floor of my office where they fell out of my pants during my ordeal with Nanette. I pick them up and Red's line goes to voicemail.

Frustrated, I call again, now on pins and needles. I had him looking into Jimmy and Nanette, not anything serious, or at least I don't feel like it's that serious. What mess could Nanette cause me? Jimmy, on the other hand, might have more of a risk associated with him. He's a known hitman, which means lots of enemies and potential snitches— folks he's done work for. When the line rings through to voicemail again, I get nervous.

Within seconds I get a text.

Red 1:12 AM: Dom, meet me at the bookstore ASAP.

Something fishy is happening. Red wouldn't call me out this late if things were fine. The message he sent me, however, saying I should call him, worried me. I slide my Glock into my waistband and pocket my phone. With keys in hand, I head to my car. Even if this is a setup it means I'm getting closer to the root of things. Red would never betray me, which means if it is a setup, he's in danger too, and I can't leave my blood unprotected.

I drive across town toward the little bookstore on Brighton Beach Avenue, owned by my family for seven generations now. Red and I have fond memories in the place, growing up as kids, reading all the smutty romance novels we could get our hands on. I smile as I turn down the street to see the lights out front turned off. Red was such a horrible influence as a kid, and I loved it. Taught me what porn is and how to find the nudey magazines my father kept in the back of the shop.

I park out front, shutting off the engine and my lights. I don't see any signs of movement inside, so I pull my Glock and chamber a round. The street is quiet too, no traffic this time of the morning, even in the city that never sleeps. I slip out of my car in silence, letting the door shut but not latch. A sweep of the street reveals nothing, not even a stray cat. It's eerie, like I'm in a horror movie gone wrong heading toward the bad guy and my inevitable doom.

"Psssst," I hear to my left, and I see Red there in the shadow waving me over. "Here, Dom."

My heart beats a little more calmly now that I know he's okay, though I'm still on edge. I keep the gun ready and duck into the dark alley. A quick glance over my shoulder tells me we aren't being followed, which is a good thing. I trust Red implicitly, but I don't have the same confidence in anyone else right now, not even my brothers. After yoyoing back and forth, I wonder if letting Sven in on this home-grown plot to oust me was a good idea. He doesn't have the same tact and wisdom as me, and I fear he may screw things up.

"Dom, we have a problem," Red says, turning around. His van—a short Mercedes Sprinter van—is parked next to a dumpster out back. One single overhead light floods the area, illuminating things enough that if someone is watching from a window of one of the nearby buildings, I will be a sitting duck. I stay out of the ring of illumination, hidden in the darkness for my own safety.

"What's going on? You're looking into Nanette Slater. Right?" I scan the area again, still feeling ill at ease, but Red's okay. That was what I feared the most. I safety my weapon and slide it into my waistband.

"Yeah, well it's not the lady that's the problem. It's her brother." Red runs a hand through his ratty hair—ginger-colored, and the reason he has the nickname. I keep my cool, refusing to show my hand as Red spouts off details about Jimmy I already know. "He says you are paying him to sniff out a mole in the family. Says you've already given him some cash, and that you've taken his sister. He was snooping around the bookshop. I caught him on camera and tracked him down, Dom. He's a serious threat. He's a hitman, and if he was hired by the Italians, we have a whole other problem to deal with."

I nod slowly. My trust in Red is firm; I have to remind myself of this. I have no reason to doubt that his motives are altruistic; he's like a brother to me, more so than my own brothers. So, if he isn't ruffled by Jimmy's confessions enough to put a bullet in Jimmy's brain himself, then he must trust Jimmy somewhat.

"What did he say?" I lean against the brick wall of the bookshop. I want to know if Red has been able to scare more information out of the rat. If Jimmy is holding out on me then we are going to have words.

"Not much else. He says you hired him and that he will only talk to you. Says he has intel and that he's valuable—too valuable to shoot." Red brandishes his own weapon, a Smith and Wesson nine-mil. "We can't risk people like him knowing about the family, Dom. And Sven knows too. Sven is on to this Jimmy guy like stink on shit. I'd have called him, but I figured I'd give Jimmy the benefit of the doubt until you got here."

He chambers a round and nods at the van. "I have him here. I can finish the job if you want, or you can question him first."

I raise my hand, waving off Red's vengeant protectiveness. "It's okay, Red. I did hire him." It's time to put the chips on the table for Red, bring him in the circle. It will wound me greatly if I have to harm him because he doesn't trust me as much as I trust him, but I have to find out who opened the door to this evil my family has suffered, both the plot on my life and the one against my mother.

"What?" he asks, squinting in confusion. "Why didn't you just call me?"

Red backs up a step. I can see he's hurt, but I don't have time to coddle feelings. "Do you want to put Sven down? Leo, Matty, Rome?" I list off my brothers first before hitting home. "Tino?" When I say Red's brother's name his eyes grow wide. "Someone in our family has hired the Italian to come after me."

"No..." He shakes his head in disbelief. "They wouldn't... The man who hurt your mom?" I hear the emotion in his voice and nod.

"If I have to put them down myself I will, but I hired an outsider because I can't imagine asking you or any other member of our family to kill one of our own. The pain will be bad enough when we learn who it is." I squeeze his shoulder and give him a stern look. "Let Jimmy out."

Red sighs, holstering his gun and nodding. "Yeah, Dom." He moves toward the van, unlocking it before sliding the door open. Jimmy lays there trembling like a fool. He has been crying, probably thinking he's going to be executed or something. I tear the duct tape off his mouth, and he instantly pleads for his life.

"Woah, Dom, please. Don't kill me. I swear, I was just looking for information about the mole. Please..."

I grab him by the arm and drag him out of the vehicle until he's in a pile on the street. Red pulls out his pocketknife, opening it, and Jimmy's trembling sobs grow louder.

"Shut the fuck up before you wake someone," I tell him, stepping back into the shadows by the dumpster.

Red slits the ties on Jimmy's wrists and ankles and lets him go free. He is instantly on his feet backing away from Red with a frantic look. Red has a scowl, but he says nothing. It's alright; I'll deal with that later. Right now, my interest is focused on Jimmy. If Red and Sven sniffed him out, it means he likely has some details for me, because it means he's been investigating.

"Spit it out, Jimmy. Tell me what you have."

His eyes flick nervously to Red then to my face. "I'm out, Dominic. I am not doing this, and you need to let my sister go. She is not a part of this."

I pull my weapon and point it right at his chest. "Tell me what you have, Jimmy."

He holds his hands up defensively. They're shaking as he backs away. "No, I'm done. Nothing else. I want no part of this. Count me out."

I gesture with the weapon, indicating Red should back away and he does. "I'm giving you one last chance, Jimmy. Say what you know now, and I'll let you and Nanette live."

"Fuck you, Dominic. Just fuck you! You can't do this." He backs another step farther away and then says, "I have it narrowed down to two men, but I'm not sure which of them it is, and I'm not pulling that trigger. I'm not winding up on your radar or anyone else in your family."

"Names, Jimmy."

"No... You swear to me you'll let Nan go, and I'll tell you."

"I swear to you that if you don't finish this job, Nanette dies. Is that what you really want? To watch her die, after you saved her all those years ago?" His face goes white as a sheet.

"What do you mean?"

"I mean the scar across your body, the one you got from Gallagher when you tried to kill him, and he was faster to the draw. I mean when he fucked your sister's little pussy and forced you to watch." I take a step closer to him. "I mean, when he nearly destroyed you... You did that to save her, to avenge her. This is your chance at redemption, Jimmy, only I'm not like Gallagher. I don't miss." My weapon still firmly pointed at his chest; he whimpers.

"Fuck you, Dominic." He glances down the alley.

"You don't have to tell me the name; just put a bullet between their eyes. That will be quite enough to let me know who it is. Finish the job, or I become the man who finishes what Gallagher started."

Jimmy takes off into the night, fleeing me and Red, and I stand there watching. I will never harm Nanette that way, but Jimmy doesn't know that. I could never harm her that way. Not now, not after she's seen me. I may never convince her that she belongs to me, is safer with me, but I can never hurt her.

"What do we do now, Dom?" Red's quavering voice beckons me, and I turn to face him.

"I need your word that anything you hear, from Sven, Leo, Nick, any of them, that you make sure I hear it. I need eyes and ears everywhere, only folks we trust. No one can know there is a mole, and no one can know about Jimmy." I stare him down and he nods abruptly.

"My life is in your hands until death, Dom. I have your back through and through." Red offers his hand to shake, and I grip it firmly.

"I know I can count on you." I'm taking a risk with this, but I have no choice now. It's either trust Red with my secret or end up killing him with my bare hands. "I'm going home. Follow Jimmy. See where it leads. Call me if anything turns up."

I head to my car and then home. I'm exhausted but restless. I need answers, but right now I need her more. To feel her body cradled in mine, where I know she's safe. Nanette has become my substitute, the one whom I've focused all my vengeant emotions around protecting. I sneak back up the stairs, laying my weapon, wallet, and keys on the nightstand before I strip off my slacks and shoes, tossing my shirt to the floor with them.

In just my boxers, I crawl into bed with her. She wakes slightly as I shake the bed and rolls to face me with sleepy eyes. "Are you okay? Where did you go?"

After last night's performance I'm surprised she is still speaking to me. "I'm fine. Family business."

I don't give any more answers, but she knows what my family is now. She doesn't ask for more details, and she doesn't shy away when I pull her against me tightly. Her breathing is shallow, thready, as if she's frightened. So I whisper, "I'm not going to hurt you, Nan." I kiss the back of her head and she relaxes in my embrace. "It's almost over now."

And it is, because one way or another I need to end this before I go insane.

16

NANETTE

I sit on a bench surrounded by flowers, wisteria in bloom dangling from the arbor, peonies and lilies cloaking the small garden oasis in bright colors and scents. But I'm tormented. Dominic has no idea what he's done to me, what he opened up when he stole my power from me. I've barely slept. I haven't eaten a bite. Nightmares keep me awake at night, and flashbacks keep me terrified during the day.

I stare into the fountain, water splashing at my feet occasionally as the breeze picks it up and tosses it at me. I'm numb, paralyzed with the same emotion I learned to stuff away more than a decade ago, but it's all back now. Like he uncorked a bottle of champagne after having shaken it up. Nothing is safe, not even sleep anymore. And Jimmy... I've asked Dominic several times how my brother is, but he doesn't answer. It's like he's trying to forget where I came from. Like he's traded me and my trauma for his mother and hers. I am now a substitute for the pain he endured in his life, and he controls everything I do in the hopes that he can stop something from happening to me.

All he did was make it worse. I was fine. I was coping without his interference, and now because he knows, because he's had the gall to announce his knowledge of my past, I'm trapped.

I close my eyes, trying to push away the racing thoughts, but as I do I see red. Only red. The blood pours from Jimmy's chest. It's on his hands, on his clothing. It streams down around him into a puddle of more blood on the carpet beneath him, his life force slowly soaking into the Berber of Gallagher's office. I hover over him, also caked in blood, screaming his name.

"Jimmy! Please, someone!" I cradle his head, watching him bleed out. He's here in my arms but I feel lost, like he's going to die and there is nothing I can do to save him. Gallagher stands over me with a gun in hand, still smoking.

"Your brother got a little too feisty, Nanette. You need to warn him of what I'm capable of doing to him. My sort of money and power don't come cheap and I make friends too, lots of them. Jimmy is going to regret this." He holds his cheek, right where Jimmy punched him.

I feel such unchecked hatred wash over me. I want to rip Gallagher apart with my hands, making him pay for the crime he committed against Jimmy. However, there's nothing I can do; no matter how hard I try, there's no way around his strength and power.

The room is spattered with blood. Jimmy is slumped on the floor, a pool of red forming around his chest wound. I squeeze my pocket handkerchief in my clenched fist as I crouch by him and press the fabric onto the wound, but it does nothing; it only soaks up the scarlet liquid within seconds. I'm shaking, breaths coming out in sharp pants as I frantically search for a way to save Jimmy, yet all options seem lost.

Gallagher stands there with a twisted smile, taking delight in my desperation and misery. I open my mouth for an angry retort—pleading for his mercy— but abruptly stop myself; he has already made up his mind, and death was what awaited Jimmy regardless of anything else. He wants Jimmy to suffer.

"You monster!" I scream at Gallagher. I hate him. I hate his office; I hate his face. I want him to die, not Jimmy. I glare at Gallagher, his face twisted in a contemptuous sneer, as if he's relishing this moment. I can't bring myself to speak, my anger pulsing through me like electricity, and my body shaking with rage.

He calls someone on his phone, mumbles something into the receiver and leaves. I sit there, naked, with Gallagher's body fluid still leaking out of me, while Jimmy is dying. I sob harder, wishing I could stop this. My brother needs me. He tried to defend my honor, protect me from this sick bastard, and this is what happened? Yes, Jimmy had a knife, but he didn't use it. He only punched the man, and now he could die.

"Please help!" It seems like hours pass. I have no concept of time. I only watch the blood pool grow, spreading beneath both of us now. There is a hole in Jimmy's stomach. I plug it with my finger. "Please, Jimmy, don't leave me." I plead with him to stay, even as his eyes flutter shut. Mom and Dad left; he's all I have. I can't lose him.

"Nanette?" I hear Dominic's voice call me and instantly I sober. I wipe my eyes, hoping he hasn't seen me crying, and I sit straighter on the stone bench. The garden has been my refuge for the past few days rain or shine. He knows I'm here; he's the one who told me to come here. He said it helps him think straight. All it's done for me is to remind me of how much I want to leave this place, find Jimmy, be safe again.

"Nan?"

"Here," I call, squirming. I sniffle quietly and wipe my eyes one more time just as Dominic rounds the corner.

He pauses, watching me. A look of angst crosses his features, disapproval maybe or perhaps frustration? He can't possibly think I'm okay, not with what he knows about me. Not after he stole my power. I explained this to him, but he still expects me to swallow the trauma and be alright, or maybe he just doesn't know how to help. Maybe watching his mother suffer for so long before she killed herself left him feeling as powerless to help me as I feel about helping myself.

He walks over and sits on the bench next to me, staring at the fountain. The small cherubs out of whose mouths the water flows seem to taunt us, provoking memories I don't want, though I can't speak for Dominic.

"Jimmy discovered the person who is at the heart of this attack on my life. I have to play my cards right, or rather he does." He talks to me as if I'm his confidant, someone he can place trust in. This is new to me. "He says it's one of two people, and I have a feeling I know who."

"What are you going to do?" I ask, keeping my gaze trained on the water-spewing cherubs. Their white stone eyes penetrate my thoughts, prying me apart as if inside of me I hold the key to making them alive.

"I'm going to find out who it is and I'm going to kill them."

I look away from the fountain, turning to Dominic who keeps his eyes facing forward. "It is what I have to do."

I swallow hard. I knew he was a killer; I just didn't think he would be so open to confess to me. Maybe it's because I've seen him, the room, his scar. He feels vulnerable with me too. It makes me wonder what the hell is happening. Why is the most powerful man in organized crime confiding in me? Who am I to him?

"How can you be so cold, so calculated?"

His eyes turn to meet mine and he stares at me, a haunting, empty stare. All I see is anger and pain in those eyes. They've witnessed things, done unspeakable atrocities, and yet I'm not afraid now.

"Someone raped my mother, Nanette." His jaw clenches and his nostrils flare. Then he continues. "I tried to stop them. I did what I could, but I was only a boy. The scar... he did that to me."

I remember the scar on his chest. It looked like whoever had cut him had nearly sawn him in half. It is an awful wound, and I can only imagine how badly it hurt, how much blood there was. It looked far worse than the wound Jimmy got. I say nothing and he continues his story.

"Months went by, and she never left her room. Months turned into years. Her pain was too much, too great. The attack was retribution from one of my father's enemies, or so I was told. Until recently I still believed that. I was ruthless, watching over the family business to ensure we buried any of our enemies who rose up." His head drops and I look away, ashamed to witness his grief like this.

"She killed herself, Nanette. The torment of what happened was too much. She couldn't process it. And I am the one who found her there. I used to go read to her, magazines, stories, even medical journals. Then she was gone, and I was alone." Dominic stands and walks across the path, gently touching a vine of wisteria.

"I'm sorry that happened." I don't know what else to say. I know the pain his mother endured. I live it out every night in my nightmares, worse now than before I met him, but every night all the same. I've watched him agonize for several days now, tormented by the revelation he has now shared with me, that he may know who is behind his mother's attack and the one planned for him. I understand that torture, and something inside of me drives me to my feet. I walk over to him and stand next to him, watching the bees flutter around the violet-colored flowers.

"Will you help me?" I ask, hesitant. Asking a man like Dominic for help is dangerous. It will lead to regrets. I'm certain of that. But I want revenge. If he has been able to learn everything about his mother and can now, years later, avenge her, maybe he can help me get the justice I seek.

"Kill a judge?" he scoffs, looking at me out of the corner of his eye. "You want me to help you kill a judge. Are you insane?"

I shrink back, hurt by his insinuation that I don't know what I'm doing. "No, I'm not. I'm angry and hurt, and I deserve justice like your mother." I cross my arms over my chest. "You've killed far more powerful people than a judge. I know your type, Dominic. You can't fool me."

"You haven't though." He plucks a strand of wisteria and holds it to his nose. "The most beautiful and delicate things need to be protected, not tarnished."

"What the hell is that supposed to mean?" I'm upset now, ready to walk off his property and never come back. I want help, not some symbolic lecture that is meant to teach me a lesson I won't ever figure out.

"It means, you don't want to be like me, Nanette. If you kill Gallagher, you become like me. I'm cold, brutal, angry. My heart has no soft spots, only edges. When I cut someone, they bleed. And when that happens, I don't shed a single tear." He tosses the wisteria to the ground and stamps it out like a lit cigarette. "Pretty things get crushed."

"I hate you; you know? Why the hell did you bring me here, expose my secrets, trash my fucking heart, and lead me to believe you were going to help me? You have no soul." I turn and start to walk away, and he is there, snatching my wrist.

"You don't get to walk away from me."

"The hell I don't!" I yank my arm away and keep walking. The path leads up to the house, and from there I can dip around the property to the front where I can find a sidewalk and head home. I don't have to stay and put up with this.

"You are going to regret that." Dominic is on me again, this time grabbing my elbow. I turn around, jamming my hand hard into his ribcage, but it hurts me and doesn't even knock his breath away.

"Fucking let me go."

"You agreed to come here, to protect Jimmy." His eyes stare into mine from inches away and I'd like to smack him.

121

"You can't control people."

"Funny, it looks like I am." His grip tightens, making me wince.

"Ouch!" I snarl. "Is this what you do? You just hurt people because you can't control them, make them want to be around you? What about Jimmy? Have you hurt him? Will he live to tell the story of how he stood up to you?"

"You're pushing the limit!" he shouts, and a few birds flutter out of the bush near us, startling me. I jerk, leaning into him in fear, then immediately realize what I've done. I push away from him and try to free myself, but his grip is too tight.

"It's touching that you think you can protect me from myself, but one day I will kill Gallagher, even if I go to prison for it. The man ruined my life and Jimmy's. He is the reason Jimmy is who he is today." I claw at his fingers. "The reason Jimmy's life is now being threatened by you. Because you're a beast, horrible and ugly and out of control."

"I'll help you," he says, his voice steely and cold. I pause, not sure I hear him right.

"You'll what?"

"I'll help you kill Gallagher, but you have to stay here." He stares down his nose at me as I slowly swallow and nod.

"Under one condition..." His grip loosens ever so slightly.

"What's that?"

"That you make sure Jimmy is safe when this is over. That you don't let anything happen to him." I shake as I say the words. I will kill Gallagher. I won't let anything happen to my brother, but some things are out of my control. Hopefully they aren't out of his though.

"I can't make promises."

"Then fucking let me go. I'm not staying." I yank my arm away successfully, but before I even turn, Dominic's hands are on my waist. He pulls me backward against his chest and whispers into my ear.

"You convince Jimmy to get this job over with, and I'll give you what you want." His breath is hot on my cheek, and I'm not certain this is the right move. I want to believe him, but I don't. Men like him aren't exactly trustworthy.

I nod and he turns me to face him. "Swear it," I tell him, looking up into his eyes defiantly. "Swear that Jimmy will be okay, and that Gallagher will die."

"Men who follow orders have no need to be afraid of me."

I can't help it. I'm overwhelmed with gratitude, and I throw my arms around his neck. The center of all of my pain for more than ten years unleashes in that moment. I kiss him hard, pulling myself up, and he lifts me as I wrap my legs around his hips. The embrace is intense; I almost can't breathe. His arms hold me so tightly he's crushing me, but I won't have it any other way.

"You swear to me, I'll get my revenge and my brother lives?" I ask again as he turns and carries me back toward the bench.

"I don't say things I don't mean," he mumbles against my mouth. Then he bites my lip, nearly drawing blood. His hands are greedy, demanding, pawing at my body as he walks.

"He needs to be punished.… You know? For what he did to me and Jimmy…" I am panting now, pulling at his shirt. The hem pulls up out of his waistband and I tug it upward.

"He'll be punished. I don't make mistakes."

Dominic is so confident and assertive; I can't help myself. He sets me on the bench, and I cling to him, kissing him and pulling his shirt up over his head. I've never wanted to feel someone against me so badly as right now. His promise, his confidence., they drive me wild. I'm finally going to get my revenge, and from a source I least expected it. When Dominic taunted me at that restaurant, I thought he was the enemy, that Gallagher had come back to get me again.

I was wrong.

Jimmy was wrong.

I stand on the precipice of the thing I've needed my entire adult life— revenge—and this man, who I wanted to hate, is going to help me get it. "Fuck, Dominic, I can't believe you're going to help me."

"I keep my word. Now, take your clothes off…"

17

DOMINIC

I stand over Nan as she slowly unbuttons her shirt and lets it slide down her arms. She's different this time, not angry or demanding with me. I slowly unbuckle my belt and step out of my shoes. My cock is swelling, filling out nicely in anticipation of burying itself in her.

"You always leave me wanting more," I say to her as I lower myself toward the bench. "I should have you locked up in a cage with nothing but my cock." She rises and shoves her slacks down, kicking them off. Her panties are gone too, removed and left inside her pants.

"You want me?" she whispers, looking away from me.

"Yes," I breathe.

"Show me."

The only thing remaining is her bra, but seeing her creamy, round tits framed in by the red silky material is hot. I think I'll leave it for a moment.

I slide my pants down my thighs and move Nan's body to the edge of the bench. I use my thumb and forefinger to pull my cock out of my boxers and step toward her. Her wetness is glistening on her lips, begging me to dip my fingers in. She meets me halfway, pressing her lips to mine and wrapping her arms around my neck. I wrap my hand around the back of her head and play with her hair as we kiss. Then as I kneel, I use both hands to spread her lips and examine her clit before taking it into my mouth. She gasps and squeals as I suck on it and run my tongue just under the hood.

I love the way she tastes, like a woman ready to be fucked. I slide my fingers in and out of her with my thumb pressing down on her clit. She's arching her back and begging for more.

"Please, Dom, fuck me," she begs. It's one of the first times she uses my name shortened the way the others do, and I love it. I also love the way her voice shakes when I'm inside her, so I thrust harder, massaging her nub in a tiny circle.

"Oh, I'm going to fuck you, so hard you can't walk." I really work her pussy, thrusting my fingers into her as she grabs my wrist and urges me to go faster.

"Fuck yeah," she moans as she's talking, "yes, like that."

"Harder? You like it rough, don't you, you little vixen." If I plunge my fingers into her any harder, I'll bruise her insides, but she seems to love it, so I let her have it.

"Yes, yes, fuck, fuck, fuck!" she screams as her body tenses and her juices pour out onto my hand. She's coming, and I can feel her muscles twitching and fluttering around my fingers as she grips the wood with both hands now. Her mouth hangs agape, eyes shut, and her pussy contracts around my fingers. It's a powerful sensation, knowing I do this to her.

When her body relaxes, and her tremors stop, I pull my fingers from her ripe slit and suck them clean. She lifts her head, eyes hooded with lust, and grins at me. "Now, give me your dick," she says in a sultry voice.

She's already wet, so I can slide in deep and get right to fucking her. The bench isn't exactly made for fucking, so I'm practically laying on top of her, pounding my cock into her eager pussy. She's still coming down from her orgasm, and I'm working up to mine, so those two things make it easier for me to focus on fucking her.

As I fuck her, I pull her bra down to expose her breasts. Her dark pink nipples are so hard and erect that my cock twitches in response. I flick my tongue over one of her tits, latching on tight and taking her whole areola into my mouth. I don't suck on it, not yet. I just let it sit there and enjoy the feel of her skin. I kiss it, nibble on it, and lick all around it until I can't take it anymore. Then I bite her. Not hard enough to leave a mark, but hard enough so she knows I'm there, and I'm not going to be gentle. I want her to remember this, to remember me.

I thrust into her slowly at first, pulling back and sliding back in. She's so tight around me, I feel like I could come already, but I hold off. I'm not going to last long at this rate, but I don't want to come yet. I want to be inside of her forever. Her pussy clenches around me and I shudder, gritting my teeth against release.

"God, your dick is huge," she pants, clawing at my hips. Her hands search my sides eagerly, scraping and scratching my skin.

I thrust harder, faster. I want to feel my cock press hard against her back wall. I want her to have to work to take it all. I'm almost there. Her pussy milks me so good; I know I'm going to blow soon.

"Oh, you're going to make me come," I pant. "Are you going to come with me, Nan?"

"Yes," she groans. "Yes, I'm going to come." Her clit is swollen and tender, but it doesn't stop her from rubbing it. I like the way she's being so aggressive, and I give her a hard kiss as I pull out.

My cock is wet with her juices, and I want to keep it that way. I scoop up some of her juices and rub it into my cock.

"More?" I ask, moving my cock up and down her pussy.

"Yes, yes," she moans, dragging her fingers down my chest. She's crazy, pushing her hips against my body, letting her moisture smear over my dick and hips. It's hot, and the fact that she isn't even hindered by being outdoors for this is even hotter.

"You are a bad girl, Nanette," I tell her, pinning her hips down. I tease her entrance with the head of my dick, slowly rocking my hips. She whimpers.

"God, just put it back in me," she moans, scratching as she pulls my hips hard. I don't think she's trying to hurt me, but part of me wants her to. That's the part of me that wants her to mark me, to leave a sign that I was here. She arches her back, taking me deeper as I push into her again. I love the way her pussy wraps around my cock, the way it massages me, and the way she moves beneath me.

She's breathing heavily, whispering my name as she comes. I'm not far behind her, and I feel my balls contracting as I thrust harder and faster. Her low moans become frantic, high-pitched screams, and her nails puncture my skin. "That's it, scream. Tell the whole world you are mine now." I thrust harder, feeling her body slam against mine. Her pussy takes it, welcoming me into its pulsing cavity. "You'll never fuck another man, Nanette. You're mine now. You belong to me."

"Fuck, fuck...." She groans, and she lets her head drop to my chest, but I'm not finished. I slow my pace for a moment, controlling the need for release. I even stop, letting her warmth surround me as I kiss her, gripping her head in my hands.

"You're mine. Did you hear me? Mine." I force her to keep her head up and as her eyes blink open, she licks her lips.

"No one owns me," she whispers, breathless.

"I own you, and it is the freest you'll ever be." I kiss her hard again, biting her lip then letting her head go. A low growl emanates up out of my chest as I begin thrusting again. I'm so close now, I know I can't hold back.

"Come for me," I growl as I thrust hard and deep. It doesn't take long, and I feel her pussy contract as I shoot my load into her. I let out a low guttural moan as I come, my teeth sinking into her shoulder as I fill her with my cum.

My head is spinning, and I'm not sure if I'm going to pass out or not, but I know that I don't want to stop. I don't want to pull out of her, and I don't want this feeling to end. It's so hot, so dirty, so animalistic. It's exactly what I need right now. She's still panting, trying to catch her breath, and looking at me like she wants more. I shiver as her lips trail over my skin as I slowly stand and watch my cum drip from her pussy to the soft grass below. I reach down and yank her up so that she's standing in front of me.

Looking down at her, I feel a swelling in my chest, a feeling of pride. She's mine, and she'll only ever be mine. Her body is slick under my touch, dampened with sweat from our workout. She looks up at me still with a lust haze in her eyes. We stand wrapped in each other's arms. I'm not ready to admit that she is my weak spot. If I do that, someone will come after her, try to hurt her. I can't let that happen.

"What did you mean by I belong to you?" Her innocent question comes as she begins straightening her bra, tucking her tits back into it. I bend and pick up her panties and slacks and hand them to her.

"Exactly what I said, you belong to me. No one else is ever going to touch that pussy of yours. You're mine."

She straightens and looks away, as if there are yet reservations inside of her. She'll come around, especially when I show her what it means to belong to me, how I treat those who belong to me.

"Are you saying you want to marry me? Are you in love with me?" She sits on the bench, holding her clothing in hand, watching me dress. They are fair questions, but one's I can't answer. Not now.

"You ask a lot of questions. Just be thankful it's me claiming you and not someone else far more sinister than me." I buckle my pants then my belt and wait for her as I put my shirt back on and slide my feet into my shoes. She dresses painfully slowly, as if comprehending everything I've said.

When she is dressed, shoes in hand, I offer my arm and we walk back toward the house. She is quiet and I don't speak either. I never expected Nanette to blast into my life like a wrecking ball, but here she is. As we reach the house, I open the door for Nanette and lead her to the living room where I pour us each a glass of whiskey. We sit in silence for a few minutes, sipping our drinks. I can feel her eyes on me, studying me.

Finally, she speaks. "So, what's next?"

I take a deep breath and set my glass down. I've always been a lone wolf, doing things my own way without anyone to answer to. But now, with Nanette in my life, I have someone to protect and provide for. And that means I have to be careful, especially in this line of work. I hesitate for a moment before answering. I've never been good at relationships, and the idea of being tied down to just one person is a foreign concept to me. But something about Nanette makes me want to hold onto her, to keep her close.

"Next, you go to your room and stay there. The door will be repaired later today. I'll get you after dinner. I need you to make Jimmy work. It's out of my hands now." I sip my whiskey and watch her face shift.

"What do you mean it's out of your hands now?" she asks, watching me over the rim of her glass. Her eyes grow wide in fright—a healthy thing.

"My brothers know about Jimmy." I hold a steady gaze in her direction, but my mind is wandering. "If you don't convince him to finish this, they'll take matters into their own hands, and I won't be able to stop them. My cousin has already picked him up once for snooping around."

"That can't happen. You promised—"

"Enough," I snap. Nanette stands, frightened. "I will do what I need to do to protect what is mine. Now, you go rest. We have to get you in to see Jimmy and make him start working with me instead of against me. His life depends on it. And if they connect him back to you, I'm going to have a mess on my hands."

She nods, clutching her whiskey glass in hand as she walks over to the liquor cabinet and fills it to the brim. She's shaken and I know why. She's terrified of losing her brother, and she should be. I dragged him into this and now with the way I feel about her, I have to make sure I do my part to get him out of this.

I watch her walk toward the door and pause, looking over her shoulder. "Dom?" she asks, her voice nearly a whisper.

"Yeah."

"Gallagher has to die…"

"I know."

She vanishes into the hallway, and I sip my drink. I'm under no illusion that things will be easy. This is the messiest the family business has ever been, and I've brought more mess to it by bringing the Slaters in. I can't—won't—let anyone touch her, but if Jimmy doesn't get his head out of his ass and do something right, he is going to die. The blame lies squarely on his shoulders, not mine, but Nanette won't see it that way.

"Sir," Mika says from the doorway, "you have a call from Sven. Says it's urgent and he needs to speak with you." She waves a phone in the air, and I nod.

"Tell him I'll call him in a half hour. I'm enjoying my drink." I raise my glass and she nods, backing away. I know he's going to light me up about Jimmy and I want to be calm about it. I have to think things through before my temper gets the better of me. Sven knows someone is out for me, but neither of us know exactly who yet. For now, that remains my secret—or Jimmy's rather.

For now...

That little weasel is going to start talking or I'm going to cut his tongue out myself. No need for Sven to get involved. Either way, Nanette is mine and I won't live without her now. It's rare to find a woman who sees you for exactly who you are and doesn't shy away, even when you show her you are a beast. I am never going back to street whores ever again.

NANETTE

I dozed off earlier this afternoon, and I awake to the sound of the door clicking shut. I jerk upward, looking around the room. Dominic is here, standing by the door. He looks stern, as if something has gone wrong. His normal blue suit is replaced with black turtleneck and slacks. He looks like he's dressed to go on a stakeout or heist. But he looks good, the color black suits his complexion well.

"Time to get ready," he says, walking into the room. He moves straight for the dresser where he opens drawers and begins pulling clothing out. I rub my eyes and yawn. The afternoon nap made me a bit groggy, but I'm sure once I wake up fully, I will feel much more alert. That much whiskey always makes me pass out.

"Ready?" I ask, turning so my feet dangle off the side of the bed. I slide off, tiptoes barely touching the carpet as I stretch my arms over my head. The door is fixed, compliments of one of Dominic's men earlier, while I was still drinking. It took the man less than twenty minutes to swap the door out for a new one, frame and all.

"We were supposed to go to dinner with Jimmy, but he's refusing to see me in public. Now that my brother, and potentially the mole, knows about me hiring him he's scared. Probably a good thing. He's clumsy." Dominic rifles through my drawers—my drawers? Am I calling this my home now? I stand and walk his direction, noticing he's selected a pair of jeans and a white top, no bra or panties. Of course, I'm wearing those now, but I know how he likes to watch me dress, or undress rather.

"So where are we meeting him?" I lean on the dresser as he picks up the stack of clothing and hands it to me. I take it, waiting for him to answer. If Jimmy won't go out, then we should go to him, but if people know about him being involved with Dominic, then it probably isn't a good idea for Dom to be at Jimmy's place. It will only bring more attention to him. My goal is to keep him safe.

"You're going in alone. I'm not going. My cousin will drive you." He walks to the bed and sits down then runs a hand through his loose dark hair.

"Me alone?" I shudder with fear. "That sounds dangerous. What if someone is watching and they connect me to all of this? I don't want any part of this scheme." I hesitate, fear creeping in. I never in a million years thought I'd be playing the part of messenger for the head of the Bratva, but here I am tangled up in his life so deep I may as well be his drug mule.

"Look, Nanette, lives are on the line here. It's going to be just like any other day you visit Jimmy. You'll get a ride into the neighborhood and Red will park. You get out and walk up to Jimmy's place like normal, then tell him what I have to say."

I look away from him. I don't want him to see my fear; he doesn't like fear. So, I turn my back on him and set the clothes on the dresser while I unbutton my top. It slides from my shoulders and falls to the ground, and I pick up the clean white top Dominic has picked out. It's a polo with three buttons, a horse embroidered on the left breast.

Simple shirt for a simple job, though I wish I wasn't thinking like this. This isn't a job; it's a visit with my brother.

"You are going to do fine, Nanette."

I tug the shirt on over my head, noticing Dominic's reflection in the picture frame hanging on the wall in front of me. He's scowling, probably upset by my fear. I have to look away; I hate that he's being upset by my emotions. Why do I hate that? What on earth is going on in my brain? I should enjoy this. I shouldn't care what he thinks or feels, but I do. I care. He's gotten to me too. I knew I'd gotten to him when he told me this morning that I belong to him now, but this?

I unbutton my slacks and push them down, stepping out of them before picking up the jeans and sliding them on. They're a perfect fit, once again, and I'm still shocked at how Dominic knew I was this size.

"So, what am I supposed to say to him then?" I zip the jeans and button them, then turn around. Dominic's eyes flash with lust for a split second, probably because I was in my panties bending over in front of him. It's the last thing on my mind. I want to see Jimmy, make sure he's okay.

He bends and picks up the ballet flats I left at the foot of the bed, shoved just beneath the frame. I kicked them off when I climbed in bed to rest. There is no way he could have seen them, not with the way the blanket drapes over the foot of the bed and pooled on the floor. He had to have been watching me sleep on his perverted closed-circuit TV.

"You're going to tell him exactly what I told you in the garden earlier today. His life is in jeopardy if he doesn't finish this. The mole may very well know he's out there hunting for my potential killer. My brother Sven knows, and Red knows. Sven knew there was a mole because we suspected it after Mom's death. We've been trying to root him out ever since. But if they talked to the wrong person about Jimmy, he's in trouble—"

"You mean, Jimmy's life is at stake because you fucked up?" I cross my arms over my chest, refusing to take the shoes he is trying to hand me.

"No, Jimmy's life is at stake because he fucked up. He went snooping in places where my family has surveillance and got caught." Dominic thrusts the shoes out in my direction, and I take them, then sit beside him.

"So what? He just kills the mole, and the rest of the family backs off? Like how will he prove he killed a bad guy then and not just a member of the family? Won't the family come after him?" I shudder to think what will happen if Jimmy goes through with this. He should just leave town now before it's too late.

"I will make sure things go down how they are supposed to. When the mole is dead, Jimmy and I will have all the evidence we need to prove to my siblings and father that it was necessary. The family will be scarred but it will be in the interest of keeping us together."

I slide on one shoe then the other and rub my sweaty palms down the fronts of my thighs. I'm nervous, probably a good thing. If I was cocky, I'm certain I would end up causing problems. Something tells me that everyone in this family is always on edge, always nervous. That doesn't make for very long life expectancy, what with heart disease and stroke due to high blood pressure and high stress levels.

"One more thing," he says, reaching into his pocket. He extracts a small silver bracelet. It has one simple blue stone as a charm dangling from the chain. It's pretty, but not a fashion statement.

"What's that?"

"It's a tracking bracelet." He grabs my wrist and wraps the chain around it, fumbling with the tiny claw clasp with his giant fingers. I pull my arm away and hold it to my stomach while I pinch the clasp with my other hand and close it.

"You don't trust me?"

"I don't trust anyone, that's what guns are for." He stands and offers me his hand. I wonder if he thinks I'm going to run or if he thinks there is a chance someone will take me. Either way, the fact that he feels the need to track me means I'm valuable to him. It makes my fear heighten a bit, because if others figure out that I'm valuable to him, they will know I'm worth taking.

"Let's get on the road." Dominic leads me downstairs to the front door where a man with fiery red hair and dark hazel eyes stands waiting. He is wearing scrubby jeans and an old flannel. I'm not sure if it's a disguise or if Dom's cousin is more country than city, but he smiles at me, and it puts me at ease. "Nan, this is Red. He will be taking you to Jimmy's neighborhood. He will also be your ride back home, so you should have this."

Dominic hands me a cell phone. It's old, a flip phone with a one-and-a-half-inch screen. I scowl at it and look up at him as I take it. "What's this for? Where is my cell phone?"

"You don't need yours. It's traceable. This is to call Red or me if there is an emergency. You can also call him when you need to be picked up. There are only two numbers programmed." Dominic taps the phone and eyes me sternly. "Every call made from this is recorded, so no funny business either. You know Jimmy's life depends on it."

I roll my eyes. "I know."

"Ready?" Red asks, gesturing to the car that sits only a few paces away outside the front door. I nod at him and glance at Dominic.

"What happens if this goes wrong? If something goes down and Jimmy is hurt. You made me a promise." I pause, hovering midway between the door and the car.

"I keep my promises. You keep yours." Dominic clasps his hands in front of himself and watches me as I finish my journey to the beat-up Toyota Camry. Red opens the door and I climb in, one last look back at Dominic as Red walks around the car and gets in.

We're off and I'm alone with this man I've never met before. It's not new to me; my occupation requires me to be with new men I've never met before on a regular basis, but not men like this. Not men like Dominic's family. At least, none that I ever knew of. Now I wonder who I've been "escorting" the past several years and if I've been in bed with other members of organized crime families.

"So, you're his cousin?" I ask the man driving. He glances at me out of the corner of his eye and nods. The silent type, that's okay. I don't mind a man who has little to say. I don't have much to say either. It makes the fifteen-minute drive across town to Jimmy's neighborhood go by easier. I have time to play what I'm going to say.

It isn't until we are parked two blocks away from Jimmy's place that I realized Dominic never blindfolded me this time. He must really mean it when he says I'm his now. He has no intention of letting me go. I find that both comforting and terrifying as Red turns the engine off. I'm still scared, fingers trembling as I unbuckle my seatbelt.

"Just get in, get the job done, and get out." Red's voice is calm. I don't get a read on what his personality is like, but I assume he's a lot like Dominic, dark, angry, brooding. I assume his whole family is that way.

I nod and open the door. Just another visit to Jimmy's place, right?

I fiddle with the bracelet as I shut the car door and begin walking. I want to glance around, see if there are any suspicious vehicles, anyone watching me, but I assume that is why Red is there in the car. He's watching me because Dominic told him to. It's why Dominic can't be here; someone would see and kill him. So, he sent his cousin in his place.

I cross the street; Jimmy's place is only three houses down the next block. I'm both anticipating a giant hug and ready to give him a massive knock to the head. Jimmy gets us both into a lot of shit and this time it's bad. I just hope he listens to reason. Dominic told me exactly what to say to him, and I have no intention of saying it. If

Jimmy makes this hit, he will have the Bratva on his tail for decades. No, I want Jimmy out of this city, and I want him gone now. Then I want Dominic to help me get my revenge on Gallagher, and I'll join Jimmy elsewhere.

Before I even open Jimmy's front door, I know something is wrong. The damn cat bowls are back. He's feeding the strays again. And next to them is a pile of trash bags and several empty liquor bottles. I bang on the door but there is no answer, so I just walk in. Not even locked. Jimmy is making mistakes, huge mistakes. If his front door isn't even locked, he's either given up completely and he's waiting for them to come kill him, or he's skipped town.

"Jimmy?" I call, moving down the hallway. I hear movement in the kitchen, a chair scooting across the linoleum. Then I see a shadow on the wall as I approach. The house smells like body odor and rotting food. "Jimmy, it's Nan. I'm here…"

I round the corner into the kitchen and see him frantically clearing lines of cocaine off the table into his palm. He looks up at me, eyes wide with surprise and stutters out a few syllables before sweeping the rest of the drugs into his palm.

"Jimmy, what the fuck? Cocaine?" I charge over to him and grab his wrist, forcing him to the sink where I dump the contents into the dirty dishes and turn the water on to rinse his hand off. He doesn't even resist me; he never would. I'm his protector, the only one who watches out for him. "What are you doing?"

"Nan, I…"

"My god, you have the mafia after you and you're snorting coke?" I leave him there washing his hands while I search the kitchen. His usual spots—old coffee can on top of the microwave, a hole in the floorboard beneath the sink, and taped beneath the kitchen chair—are all void of more drugs. "Where is it? Where is your stash?"

I eye him angrily, not even to my message from Dominic yet, or rather, my warning to get the hell out of town.

"No, Nan, I need it. Please," he pleads, grabbing a towel to dry his hands.

I march off down the hall toward the bathroom where I know he hides more drugs. I lift the toilet tank lid and hit the jackpot. Submerged in the water of the tank are two small Ziplock bags, weighed down by rocks. I flush the toilet thus draining the tank and pluck out the bags. "You really thought you'd get away with this? You know this stuff fucks you up! You knew I'd come back and find this. It took you three years to get clean last time you did this." I peel open the first bag and pour its contents into the swirling water of the toilet bowl and Jimmy snatches up the other baggie. The way he's acting, I can tell he's already going to struggle to give it up again.

"You can't come into my house and do this." He clutches the baggie in his fist, and I pry his fingers open.

"The hell I can't. Give it to me," I order, tearing the baggie. The white powder starts to trickle out, floating into the air. I manage to get it away from him and its contents get flushed along with the previous bag's stash. "What are you thinking?"

I push past him into the living room. I'm livid. He follows along, whimpering and not making much sense. These bastards have him terrified. I knew this would happen. He's a smart man, good at what he does, but this is too much. Gallagher at that restaurant triggered something in him and he's relapsing hard.

"Jimmy, did you finish the job?"

"No. I can't do it." He shakes his head, grabbing handfuls of his hair.

"They're going to kill you. Dominic and his brothers are going to kill you if you don't do the job. You either have to finish it or get out of town. That's what you have to do." I want to smack some sense into him, but I can't be angry with him. I'm just as terrified and he is handling it about as well as anyone else.

I move toward him, reaching for him to pull him in for a hug and I hear gunshots. My instinct is to drop to my knees. The shots are so loud it shakes the walls. I crawl to the window, looking out over the street. From this vantage point I can't see anything. So, I crawl past the window and stand, peeking out in only one direction. I see Dominic's cousin staggering. He falls, clutching his chest. Three other men surround him; one of them kicks him. Then they look up at the house, as if they can see past the curtain behind which I hide.

Fear paralyzes me. I look to where Jimmy was standing, and he's gone. I hear the back door slam shut and frantically head that direction. I don't know if these men are Dominic's men or enemies, the mole perhaps? All I know is my ride back to Dom's house isn't going to work out if the driver is dead in the street. I turn at the hallway, hooking around toward the back door and something trips me up. I hit the ground hard, slamming my head on the wood flooring.

"Well well, if we don't have the pretty little bitch right here." A man's voice hits my ears, making my skin crawl. I try to blink my eyes open, but someone pulls something over my head and ties it around my neck. I can still breathe but my hands shoot to my throat instinctively. I scream.

"Let me out! You can't do this." I kick and swipe at the air, hoping Jimmy got away. I feel myself being hoisted off the ground and slung over someone's shoulders while male voices talk and laugh as if they are just out for a stroll at the park, not kidnapping and murdering.

This didn't go at all as planned. And now I realize why Dominic put that bracelet on my arm. I only hope they don't realize it's there.

19

DOMINIC

The minute Nanette gets in that car I know something is going to go wrong. I can feel it in my gut and my gut is never wrong. I watch Red pull down my long drive and turn off onto the road, then I retreat into the house. The tracking chip I put into the bracelet will tell me where she is at all times, so for now I head for the kitchen. The app on my phone knows the pre-planned route to Jimmy's house, and it will chime if the tracking bracelet does not follow that prescribed path.

Mika is busy polishing silverware when I walk in. Her polite smile greets me. "Sir, what can I do for you? Would you like a drink?" She puts the butter knife down and drapes her towel over her shoulder, gazing up at me expectantly.

"No, that's okay, but what about a snack? Have any of those delicious chocolate chip cookies?" I walk toward the counter where the cookie jar sits and she clicks her tongue, mothering me.

"Before dinner?" she asks, snickering. "Of course, I always have chocolate chip cookies for you, sir. I'll get you a glass of milk too."

I sit down at the island where I imagine Nanette has taken breakfast and lunch every day since she arrived. Mika is a wonderful cook and her personality is inviting. I wonder how much Nanette opened up to her, or how many times Mika has had to get after Nanette. As she prepares my snack, I decide to broach the topic.

"Mika, you've seen our guest around here lately, cooked for her, cleaned up after her."

"Yes, Sir. Ms. Nanette is a joy." She says this without turning to look at me, though I get the hint that Mika isn't being entirely truthful. I know Nanette now; she is anything but a sheer joy. She's a handful through and through.

"What sort of vibe do you get from her? And be honest with me."

Mika turns, holding a plate of cookies and a small glass tumbler full to the brim with milk. She sets them in front of me and dusts her hands on her apron. She looks thoughtful, as if she needs to word things correctly to avoid upsetting me. I'm a stern man and all of my staff know this. I appreciate the care she puts into her response.

"Well, Sir, Ms. Nanette is opinionated. She is strong-willed, and that's a good thing for you, Sir. She will need that if she stays here long." Mika tilts her head a bit. "She's too curious. If you don't intend to reveal yourself to her fully, you need to reinforce some doors." She chuckles and pats my hand. "You like this woman?"

I look into the warm brown eyes of the woman who nearly raised me, not that my mother wasn't a good mother, but given her circumstances, Mika was the one there for me the most. I insisted she stay on when Dad moved out and left the place to me. I'd be lost without her. Besides, she knows the family in and out, her late husband being one of the higher ups before my time.

"I do." I smile at her and take a bite of a cookie. It's not warm still, but it is delicious. After I wash my bite down with a swig of milk, I say, "Do you like her?" I don't need her approval, but I do appreciate her companionship. My father will never approve of Nanette; he'll call her a common whore just like the sluts from the bar. Those will be his exact words. But when he's gone, none of that will matter, and I'll be on top.

"I do," she says, grinning. "She will keep you on your toes and you need that." Mika taps her temple. "It keeps you sharp up here."

I laugh a deep hearty laugh knowing she's true. Nanette will give me a run for my money on a daily basis. I've never wanted a passive wife who gives me everything I want and fawns over me. I want a lively, high-spirited woman who can challenge me and make me think. Nanette is just that.

I hear a chime go off, and I pull my phone out. It's been less than thirty minutes and she has already deviated from the plan. "One second," I tell Mika, shoving the second half of a cookie into my mouth. I swipe up to unlock my phone and the app appears, the last one I had open. Nanette's beacon is not signaling me from Jimmy's place. She is moving, and fast—how I don't know. Her chip is showing nearly three blocks away already and heading north quickly.

I roll my eyes, heaving out a sigh. "Well, Mika, it looks like I'll have to eat the rest of these delicious cookies another time. Thank you for the company and the sweets." I tap my hand on the counter and say, "Maybe you'll add double chocolate chips next time?"

"Oh, you know I'm trying to help you watch your waistline. The doctor won't take kindly to your cholesterol going up with all these sweets." She winks at me and picks up the plate and glass. "Go on, get to work. I'll prepare a roast and potatoes for dinner."

I nod at her and walk out, heading to my office. I'm not worried about where Nanette goes. As long as she's dumb enough to keep the bracelet on her wrist, I'll be able to track her. But that thought gives me pause for a moment. Nanette knows I put a tracker in that bracelet. It's possible she's thrown me off her scent by tossing the bracelet into a moving vehicle, or worse—someone snagged her. The second thought makes my chest tighten.

I go to my desk, pull out my Glock and the extra clip, then holster it at my side. The clip goes into my pocket before I slide my knife out of my top desk drawer. Part of me is scolding myself for not just riding along with Red. She is a lot to handle. No doubt she gave him a hard time. I slide the knife into my boot sheath and walk over to my closet where I pull out another small nine-mil. I can't be too prepared for this. If it's just Nan on the run, I'll bring her back without trouble, but if someone came for her, I'll need as much firepower as I can take. So, I grab my three eighty and slide it into my waistband.

My phone rings, buzzing in my pocket where I stuffed it after seeing her chip moving across the map. I pull it out and see it's Jimmy. Nanette should be with Jimmy right now, not calling me. I swipe to answer and hold the phone to my ear to hear him going berserk.

"Oh my god, they got her. They took her and where the fuck are they going?"

"Jimmy, calm down." I can't make sense of what he's saying. It sounds like nonsense mumbling.

"They took her, Dominic. They fucking took Nanette. She's gone. Right out of my living room." He's winded; he's been running. I hear nothing in the background except silence, which means he is not in a car chasing whomever it is that took my woman.

"What do you mean they took her? Who took her?" I move toward the front door with catlike speed, racing to my car.

"Some guys in black. There were gunshots, then I ran. I thought Nanette was behind me. She wasn't. I was out the back and over the fence before they got in the house, but she wasn't with me. And now she's gone. They took her."

"Okay, stop," I said, climbing into my car. "What else do you see? Look outside."

145

Jimmy whimpers and huffs. It sounds like he's on something; he's definitely not sober. "There is some dead guy on the sidewalk in a pool of blood. At least, I think he's dead. He hasn't moved a muscle in a few minutes, and that's a lot of blood."

"Fuck," I snap, pulling out onto the road. "What does he look like?"

"I don't know. Tattoo, ratty flannel shirt. He's got red hair."

My heart sinks at his description. I know it's Red. "Get out there and check if he's alive. Now!"

I slam my foot onto the gas pedal, not even worrying about stop signs or oncoming traffic. I've driven in enough high-speed chases to maneuver these crowded city streets. After several minutes I'm halfway to Jimmy's place and he's back on the line. "He's dead, Dom. The guy is dead. They have her," he sobs, almost the same cry I had when I walked into my mother's room and found her dead. I know that cry, that dread of grief sneaking up on a soul and raping it.

"Goddammit, Jimmy. They have her because you can't do your fucking job. Finish it now, or she's going to die. You get off your ass and do what you couldn't do before, because I promise you, these folks aren't like Gallagher. Once they hurt her, they're coming for you, and they won't stop until you're dead." I hang up the call and weave through a busy intersection way faster than is legal.

My phone chimes again, the app alerting me to Nan's deviation from our plan. Now I know it isn't her; it's trouble—deadly trouble. I push the accelerator down harder as I open the app and mount my phone in the hands-free holder. The chip's beacon flashes on the map revealing whatever vehicle they have her in is still on the move. That's not good. If they were keeping her alive, they'd have gone to one of my safehouses, not out of town.

I turn down High Street, hoping to cut them off. The longer that beacon flashes, the more likely I'll figure out where they're headed. I'm still miles out from catching them, but the beacon is guiding me.

My only hope at this point is that they don't realize I'm tracking her. We've used trackers like this bracelet before, but it's not common. Usually, we place a bug on a car or the bottom of someone's shoe.

"Fuck, Nan... I'm coming." Tires squeal as I turn down an alley, bouncing so hard I almost smash my head on the ceiling of the car. I have to get to her. I promised I'd protect her, that I'd help her get her revenge, and I'm not about to sit back and let them do to Nanette what they did to my mother. Not even Sven would allow that, if he knew. I don't think he knows about Nanette right now, only Jimmy, which doesn't bode well for her. They will torture her, try to get her to cough up information on her brother.

I push the car to its limits, following the beacon until it turns toward the port. I know exactly where they're going now. They planned for me to take my fall at the port shipping yard during the gun shipment exchange, and their play failed. I slow down, knowing that drawing attention now will be a bad thing. They will be expecting me for sure. This means they don't even care that she may be tracked. She may be dead already. Their game isn't to take her to get to Jimmy. She was their target all along. They've drawn me out, lured me away from the safety of my own heavily secured home into the open. I turn down an alley, stopping the car for a moment.

I take a deep breath and blow it out, trying to think clearly. If they know Jimmy is involved like Red said they do, they could have taken him at any time, killed him, and gotten rid of his body without me knowing. They don't want him. He's too easy of a job. Nanette, however, pinned up in my home, hidden away by me, she's the real one they want because she's bait. And here I am like a moth to a flame, chasing them down. I have to think.

I pound my forehead with the heel of my hand. "Think, Dominic. Goddammit." I pinch the bridge of my nose. I can't trust anyone anymore. Red is dead, and Sven will only get us both killed. I have to go in alone, decide who it is that is against me, take them out, then break Nanette out of there—if she's still alive. It's my only option.

A little calmer, I pull out of the alley and onto the street. If I go right through the front gate, there will be an ambush waiting. If I sneak in the back, they'll have guards waiting. So, I do the only thing I can think of. I see a straight box truck parked at a filling station almost a mile out, and I stop and park next to it. The driver sits in his seat munching on some sort of food, and I climb right into the passenger door and point my gun at him.

"I am going to need you to drive," I tell him calmly. "If you do what I say, you will not be hurt at all. I just need a lift somewhere I can't take my car."

"Yeah, yeah, buddy," he says, his accent thick. "Look, you don't have to point your gun at me. I'll take you anywhere you want." He throws his food out the window and puts the truck in gear. "Where you need to go?"

"The shipping yard at the port, dock A." I lower my gun and glance around. "Got another hat somewhere?"

The man's head jerks backward. "Back there," he says, indicating the six inches of space behind his seat. I turn over my shoulder and see a ball cap, blue with red letters on it that mean nothing to me. I slap that thing on my head and nod at the road. "Get me there quickly. A woman's life depends on it."

The man pulls into traffic and speeds up. I'd have been barreling along, but I hold my tongue, trying to be patient. If he can just get me close, he has nothing else to do. Right now, the only thing I can think about is getting to Nanette and making sure she's alive and safe. And I'll gun down anyone or anything that stands in my path. I'm on the edge of my revenge; I can taste it. Even if I have to take it myself instead of Jimmy.

The driver gets me through the gate easily, stopping a few hundred yards from the warehouse where I know my gun shipments arrive. Nan's beacon is still chiming; she, or at least her body, is in that building. I put my phone on silent and turn to the man. "I owe you a great favor," I tell him. "You look up Dominic Gusev when you get a chance. Anything I can do to help you, you name it."

"Gusev? You mean like Bratva?" His eyes go wide, and I nod.

"Anything you ever want or need; you find me and it's yours." I slip out of the truck cab and as soon as my feet hit pavement, I race to the nearby dumpster to hide. I need to collect my thoughts and make a plan. I just can't do it in the open.

2 0

NANETTE

The car bumping around left bruises on my shoulders and hips. First, they threw me in the trunk of a car, and now I'm curled up against a wall. Whatever this room is, it smells like rotten fish and mildew. It feels damp too, like someone's just had a shower or maybe we're near the port. I listen intently hoping to hear something that clues me in to where I'm at, but all I hear are the sounds of a factory—the beep of a tow motor, some machines running, and men shouting over the equipment.

I shiver; it's chilly. They haven't removed the bag from my head, but they tied my arms behind my back, so I can't remove it myself. I fiddle with the bracelet, wondering if there is some way I can signal Dominic as to where I am or if just wearing the bracelet is enough for him to find me. I hope he doesn't think I ran out on him. Given enough time with Jimmy I probably would have. We'd have gotten in his car and driven it to the edge of the city and stolen someone else's car to escape from there. Of course, I'd have been smart enough to ditch the bracelet. If I get that chance, I may still take it, or maybe not. Things with Dominic aren't that horrible.

"Well, look who's awake," a male voice says, giving me a start. I thought I was alone in this place, and I'm clearly not, or maybe he just walked in. I didn't hear footsteps though.

"What do you want with me?" I'm not stupid. I know what they want with me. They want Dominic. They are probably using me to get to him now. It's possible they know he is tracking me, that they're using me to lure him out. Or worse—they want Jimmy to hunt me down. He can't do that, but he's just stupid enough to try.

"Oh, what a feisty little bitch." I hear the footsteps now as they move closer to me. Rubber boots on this cold floor, squeaking with each step. He yanks the sack off my head, and I'm blinded by the light for a moment until my eyes adjust. It's an old office with several tall filing cabinets lining the walls. A few shelves sit to one side, covered in boxes and cleaning supplies. I still don't recognize it, but at least I can see.

There is a single window on the other side of the room above a small table covered in magazines. If this jerk leaves, I can open that window and sneak out of here. I keep my eyes on it like it's my only hope, and the man with scraggly dark hair towers over me.

"Why am I here?" I ask, not taking my eyes off the window.

"You should know by now why you're here. Shacking up with Dominic taught you nothing?" He scoffs and tosses the bag onto the desk. A few papers flutter to the ground near my feet and I glance at them. There's a logo on the upper right corner of the paper, a shipping yard off Long Island Sound. I've seen commercials for it. They accept large cargo and allow people to dry dock their boats here in winter. I know where I am. Little good that does me without a phone. I'm sure they've taken that by now.

The man stares at me with interest, as if he's trying to decide what Dominic sees in me. I feel like I'm being scrutinized like a lab of meat on a butcher's hook. I shift how I'm sitting, realizing the ropes on my hands aren't that tight. I can probably slip my hands out of them if he's not looking at me. I sit perfectly still though, not wanting the man to read my thoughts. He looks scary, broad shoulders, gun strapped to his hip. If he wanted to, he could probably snap me in two.

"Who are you?" I ask, not really expecting him to give me an answer, but I memorize his face. He has blue eyes, but they're dark and stormy. There is a scar above his right eye; looks like he was sliced open at some point. I glare at him, but it doesn't faze him.

"Who I am is none of your business." He kicks my feet out from under me and I wince. It doesn't hurt but I nearly fall over.

"When Dominic gets here, you're going to pay for this. He won't like that you're mistreating me." I am so mad I could spit on him, but I don't. I don't want to make things worse for myself.

"Ha, you're funny." He crosses his arms over his chest and glares at me. "Dominic is out. He's not the boss anymore. We're making Sven the boss."

"Why so you can push him around? What do you have on him? Is he ready to stab Dominic in the back too?"

That comment earns me a smack so hard I do fall over, knocking my head against the corner of the desk. I wince, yelping in pain, and try to sit up but he's there. He stands on my hair and crouches next to me, almost putting his knee into the side of my head. Tears burn my eyes, but I blink them away. I am not weak, and this man will not get to me. I will stay strong because I refuse to be a coward.

"Listen to me good, bitch, you're just a pawn. Nothing more. There is nothing stopping me from slitting your throat right now. I could have done it already. You're alive as a bargaining chip and nothing more."

The man's phone chimes, and he stands, backing away. I watch him pull it from his pocket and he shakes his head in frustration, then turns and walks out. For a moment I lay there, waiting for him to come back, but after a few minutes I realize he isn't coming back. At least not soon. I force myself to sit up, wriggling at the restraints on my wrists until I feel like the ropes are cutting my flesh; they may be. It hurts like hell, and they're not as loose as I hoped they were.

With a bit of effort, I'm able to work my hands under my hips then around my butt until they are hugging my legs to my chest. I'm not quite flexible enough to get them fully free, but I can at least spread my knees and see the knot is loose. At first, I try in vain to squeeze my wrists out, but then I try using my teeth to untie the knot. When that proves useless, I look around the room for some way to extract myself from this mess. There is a trash can in the corner, a cardboard box that has words written in some Asian language, a few pieces of paper still on the ground in front of me, and some sort of wooden crate with a handle.

I don't hear anyone outside the door, so I scoot across the room until I can see into the crate, and I see victory. It's an old tool kit, complete with a small saw, a pry bar, some screwdrivers, a few wrenches, and some sockets. I hit the jackpot. I scoot faster, eager to get out of these ropes and try to bust out the window.

My hips hurt, but I manage to lift one leg up and reach into the box for the saw. It's awkward trying to twist it around in my hand until the blade is up against the rope, but then I set to work. I concentrate, wiggling the saw up and down in slow determined movements until the rope begins to fray, and before long, it snaps into two pieces. The rope is still wrapped around my wrists, but with one end free it only takes a second to loose it completely and I'm standing up and stretching my aching back.

I tiptoe to the door and listen, hearing the work being done outside the door. I also hear a few male voices very close to the door, which means I can't sneak out that way, so I head back to the window. It's locked, and it's frosted too. I can't see out it. I don't think we're on a second story, but I can't just climb out if we are. And I can't bust it open either. The men outside the door would come in within seconds. So, I push the lever on the top side of the window to open and try to lift it.

It's an old window, wooden, probably swollen from misuse. It's stuck, making it twice as difficult to open. Frustrated, I push upward with all of my strength, but it doesn't budge. I examine it, glancing over my shoulder a few times to make sure no one enters the room. The tan paint slapped on this old wooden frame has painted the window shut. I'll never get it open on my own, at least not without some sort of tool, so I return to the toolbox on the floor and rifle through it. I find the pry bar but no knife or other tool to break the paint seal. The pry bar will have to work.

I return to the window, eager to apply some elbow grease. The pry bar is heavy, but it's not like I haven't used one before. I press the claw into the window near the bottom, tapping it lightly to lodge it in place. If I hit it too hard, they'll hear, so I can only hope I've done a good enough job of getting it into the wood. But when I begin to pull back on the shaft, it pops out of the wood, making a loud sound. I freeze, my heart suddenly pounding ten times faster than normal, as if I wasn't already freaking out.

For a second nothing happens. I think maybe I'll get away with it, but then the door opens, and the same scar-faced man appears. "What the hell are you doing? How'd you get loose?" He barges over to me and grabs the pry bar.

I'm terrified that he may hit me with it, so I keep my hands wrapped tightly around the shaft, not giving it up. "Let go, bitch," he shouts, pulling on it.

"No, let me go." I fight him, refusing to give it up, and he brings the back of his hand across my face, knocking me over. I fall hard against the filing cabinet behind me and slide to the ground where his boot connects to my hip, and I yelp in pain.

"Fuck, stop!" I yell, shielding my face in case he wants to hit me again. My cheekbone is throbbing, and my hip hurts. It feels like he dislocated something.

"Stupid woman. What did you think you were going to accomplish with this? The whole place is surrounded by my men. We'd have seen you in literally a minute, tops. Just sit there and wait for your brother to show up."

His words get my attention and I lower my hands. "Jimmy? What do you mean? He's coming?" I'm confused. Jimmy is working with them? Or are they expecting him to come rescue me?

"You really are stupid, aren't you? Hasn't Gusev told you anything?" The man tosses the pry bar into the toolbox, and it clangs against the other tools in a loud shrill sound that hurts my ears. I cover them briefly, shaking, then lower my hands again as I curl into a ball. He crouches again, hands draped over his knees and clasped in front of himself.

I shrink back. I don't want him to talk to me anymore. I don't want him to look at me or touch me. I want to go home. I want the safety of my risky life of sleeping with rich powerful men and feeling that release. That's what I want. Normal. My specific blend of normal that makes me feel in control.

"You're too pretty to end up like this, you know? It's a shame your brother got tangled up in this. We're going to bring him right in here to say goodbye before we gut him. You can watch if you'd like." He pushes a hair out of my eyes and hooks it around my ear and I jerk my head away.

"You're a monster. Get out of here!"

He chuckles and stands, backing away slowly, but this time he takes the crate of tools with him. Now I can't hold back the tears. They come hard and fast. I don't want to stop them. Jimmy is everything I have left; they can't kill him. I need him.

I stand and limp over to the door and bang on it, screaming like an idiot. Someone has to stop them; they can't be allowed to do this. "Let me out!" I bang on the door harder, wishing I had that pry bar now.

155

The knob won't turn, locked from the outside, and I am both scared and angry. Where is Dominic? He has to know by now that I'm not where I am supposed to be. I glance at the bracelet. Isn't this thing working? Why isn't he here?

"Let me out! Dominic is going to kill you!" I pound on the door until my hands hurt, then I open my fists and smack it, sobbing, until I can't stand anymore.

This isn't supposed to be happening. When Dominic barged into Jimmy's house that day, I wanted to protect my brother. That's it. He was going to hurt Jimmy, so I told him I'd go with him willingly, and now look at us both. I should have stood up to him, sent him away. I should have forced Jimmy to run away, leave the city.

I slide down the door crying and sit leaning against it. I want Dominic to show up and do what he promised. He fucking promised! And here I am locked up, kidnapped again, only this time it's real. This time, I'm going to die if he doesn't show up. I can feel it in my bones. I don't want to die. I want Dominic to show up.

"Please, don't hurt my brother," I scream, still bawling my eyes out. "Please, Jimmy got dragged into this by Dominic. Please don't hurt him."

I don't even know if anyone can hear me now. I stopped hearing voices outside the door. In fact, I don't hear the engine of the tow motor either, and I sniffle quietly so I can listen to what's happening outside the door. I press my ear against the metal; it's cool, and I feel vibrations from somewhere. In the distance I hear talking, but it's not close. I wipe my eyes, using the hem of my shirt to wipe the snot from beneath my nose—disgusting yes, but there are no tissues in here.

"Hello?" I say aloud, hoping someone is there. I hear footsteps. "Hello?" I call, anxious. I'm not ready for Jimmy to show up, to say good-bye. It's too soon. He's all I have.

Something slams into the door hard. It makes such a loud sound I'd swear it was a gun going off. I back away from the door, cowering in the corner by the filing cabinet where the tool crate was sitting. The bang happens again, then again. I'm shaking. "Stop! Please," I cry, curled up in a ball, hugging my knees to my chest.

I cover my ears and rock, clamping my eyes shut. I want Dominic. I want to go home!

21

DOMINIC

My phone vibrates in my pocket, and I pull it out. I'm crouching behind a dumpster that reeks of dead fish, but guards pass by here every few minutes. It's the only isolated place to hide out. I answer the phone, hissing, "What!" in a loud whisper.

"Dom, it's Jimmy. The Italian is dead."

My chest is already pumping hard enough to fuel a freight train but knowing that bit of information starts to put it at ease. "And the mole?" I ask, careful to keep my voice low. I'm so close to the end of this thing, I can't blow it by getting caught now. Jimmy did his part, at least most of it.

"His name is Nick. Has a scar above his right eye. I got that much off the Italian before I put a bullet in his forehead. Now where is Nan?" Jimmy sounds frantic, but he needs to calm the fuck down. If he comes storming in here, he'll ruin everything. This is going to take precision to extract Nanette from where I know they have her locked up. I know this warehouse like the back of my hand; it's the only logical place—the back office.

"I'm getting her, Jimmy. You need to lay low now. You'll be on every-one's radar, my family and the Italians. You need to avoid your house. Go to a park, someplace public. Make sure you don't have any blood on you."

"You think I'm stupid? Of course, I have no blood on me."

Jimmy raises his voice and I'm tempted to do the same, but I hear footsteps crunching gravel on the pavement and I hold my breath. Hal walks past, carrying his AR 15 and I'm not sure who he's working for right now. We have patrols around this building at all times anyway, but there is no telling if he's loyal to me or Nick. And now that I know it's Nick, I'll have no trouble putting him down.

"Are you there?" Jimmy snaps.

"Yes, dammit. I'm hiding." I freeze as the footsteps stop, then look over my shoulder. Hal pauses for a moment, does a sweep with his gun, then continues moving. "Look, be at my house in two hours. Bring the man's finger as proof he's dead. You'll get what's coming to you." I hang up the phone and pocket it, this time shutting it off. I don't need the buzzing from vibrations alerting anyone to my presence once I get inside.

It doesn't take me long. Following our strict schedule of guard passes, I slip into the front door between rounds. I have barely thirty seconds to get down the short front hallway to the scaffolding that overlooks the production tanks below where fish are being descaled and gutted for transport. This isn't the real job; it's just a front for the gun smug-gling, but it keeps the lights on.

Halfway down the first hallway, I slip into the men's room to hide as the guard rounds the corner to do his pass of this hall. I count to fifteen, peeking out to see his back turned toward me as I crack the door. He never suspects a thing as I step out, heading the opposite direction as him. At the end of the long hallway, just past the door to the production floor is the office. I hear Nanette crying but in the interest of not drawing any unwanted attention quiet yet, I hold my tongue. She's asking if someone is out here but if I call to her, she'll really freak out.

I try the doorknob silently, but it's locked and I don't have the key. I glance around, seeing nothing but an old wooden tool crate. Nothing in it looks helpful at picking the lock, but the weight of the crate itself may just bust the knob loose. I have less than a minute until the guard walks out of the production floor into the hallway, and with the tow motors in there no longer making their noise, I'm about to take a risk that could end my life. But I have to do it.

I pick up the crate, tools and all, and heft it over my head. When I bring it down hard on the doorknob, Nanette stops talking. I don't even waste time calling out to her. I lift the crate again, bringing it down hard again. The knob breaks slightly, dangling at an odd angle as I bring the crate down on it once more. As soon as it springs loose, I drop the crate and pull out the screwdriver, using it to pry the latch bolt out of the striker plate and the door swings inward.

I push it open hard, causing it to bounce against something, but I don't even bother looking at what it hits. Nanette is curled up in a ball against the wall with her ears plugged and her eyes clamped shut. She's shaking and I don't have time to mess around. I rush over to her, grabbing her arms.

"No," she screeches, and I cover her mouth with my hand.

"Shhh," I hiss, looking over my shoulder. "We have to get out of here."

She throws her arms around my neck, squeezing me. "Dom, where is Jimmy? They said they're going to kill him." Nanette is frantic, sobbing as I lift her into my arms in a cradle hold. I stand for a second, listening, but I can't hear anything over her sobs. "They can't kill him. You promised me you'd protect him."

"Shut up, woman," I tell her, and she silences herself. I listen again and hear shouting. Someone has heard the noise I made and they're coming. I set Nanette down, prying her arms away from my neck, and push her behind me as I turn toward the door. "I might have to shoot my way out of this, Nan. You need to stay behind me and do exactly as I say or we're both dead."

"Dom, the mole... is he here?" She clings to my back, grabbing handfuls of my shirt as I move toward the door.

"Yeah, he's here."

"Is it the man who took me?" she asks, not even trying to be quiet. It's too late to be quiet anyway. Shit is hitting the fan outside this door. I open it and peek out. There is no one in the hallway now, but I can't just make a run for it. If I do, Nanette could trail behind or be caught in the crossfire.

"Stay close to me," I order, gripping her wrist with one hand and aiming the small gun from my waistband down the hallway. We get to the door of the production floor, and I look out onto the floor where a few guards are headed my way. "Go!" I hiss, pushing her past the door. She takes off, running to the end of the hallway and I turn my back to her, backing down the hall as quickly as I can.

"Fuck, Dominic!" Nanette squeals, and I turn around to see Leo grabbing her.

"Dom?" he asks, looking confused.

"Let her go, Leo," I rasp at him, and my little brother obeys, pulling his own weapon. I know instantly he's loyal as I back toward him until we're shoulder to shoulder. Nanette twists a doorknob, but it's jammed shut, maybe locked. She frantically pulls on it, whimpering as I address Leo. "We have a mole, Leo. It's Nick for sure, maybe others. They're hunting me." It's the fastest explanation I can give without any evidence to prove it to him, but he's got my back.

"Go," he tells me, pointing his gun down the hallway. "I'll hold them off."

Nanette yelps as I push her away from the door and aim my gun at it. The moment I pull the trigger I'm going to alert them to my location, but I have to do it. I fire the gun, blasting the doorknob and the door whines as it opens. Nan is the first one through and I follow her. Leo trails us, still covering our backs, and I hear gunfire erupting in the hallway. The room has a single window that I know leads to the alley behind the building. It's where I was hiding before sneaking in.

"Get down," I tell her before using my elbow to smash the glass. Nanette drops to her knees, covering her ears as Leo fires his weapon down the hallway.

"Fuck, Dominic, it's Warren. He's literally shooting at me." Leo uses the metal door as cover as he continues unloading his gun. I pull the Glock out of my holster along with the spare clip from my pocket, and I slide them across the floor to him.

"Use this."

Leo accepts the help when his gun clicks a few times—empty of rounds. He picks up the Glock and continues watching my back. Within minutes the police will be called and arrive, so I need to get out. After that, I'll have to have my buddy at the precinct clean this mess up, but for now my concern is staying alive and keeping Nanette safe.

With my back covered, I bust the rest of the glass out of the window. Shards still protrude from the frame, so I slip my jacket off and lay it over the ledge. "Nan, we have to climb out." I tell her. The window is high, but we shouldn't get hurt if we're careful. "I'll go first." I slip my gun into my waistband and lean out the window. There are no guards. It's likely they are all being drawn inside to where the real fireworks are erupting.

"God, Joey too. Dominic, the whole place is shooting. Sven is shooting at Joey." Leo sounds frantic, as if this is a complete shock to him. Sven did a better job at hiding the plot than I gave him credit for.

"Just keep the shots coming. The ones who are shooting at you are our enemies. The more we take out, the cleaner this family will be."

"But they're all family!" he shouts, reaching out the door to fire off another round.

"Just because they're blood doesn't make them family." I gesture to Nanette to come to the window, then slide one foot out. As I swing my other foot out the window and lay across the ledge, reaching with my toes for the dumpster below, she clings to my hand.

"Fuck, you can't leave me here."

"I'm not leaving you here. Climb out the window and I'll help you down." The tips of my toes land on the edge of the dumpster. It's a precarious position but I manage to balance for the moment. I stretch into the window and reach for her, but a gunshot resounds behind me, and I feel stabbing pain in my left shoulder. I fall into the dumpster, screaming in pain.

"Dominic!" she screeches, but she doesn't look out the window. Smarter than I thought she was. It takes me a moment to get my bearings, and when I do, I sit up, ready with my gun. I peek over the edge of the dumpster and see two men approaching and a car rolling up slowly. Without a thought in my head, I call out, "This is Dominic. If you're not with me, you're against me." The men continue charging at me, which is proof enough to me that they are not friendly.

I reach over the edge of the dumpster and point my gun at them, and still, they don't back off, so I fire three rounds, the first one hitting one of the men, and the second one missing, before the third hits the second man. I take a breath, wincing in pain. If they'd hit my right shoulder, I'd be in far more danger. Lucky for me I'm right-handed.

"Nan, you're going to have to jump," I shout up at the window, and before I can even repeat the phrase, her feet are out and she's leaping on top of me. She lands with a loud crash and it's my turn to yelp in pain. I still hear gunfire rattling off inside, but I'm more worried about the car approaching now. Whoever it is has seen that both of us are in the dumpster, and we're sitting ducks. I have one round left in this gun, eight in the three-eighty, and nothing else but my knife.

"Dom, that guy driving the car, he's the one who took me." Nanette is suddenly quiet, her harsh whisper revealing her fear.

"What did he look like?" I ask, quite aware that the car is getting closer by the second.

"Scar above his right eye, blue eyes. He has scraggly brown hair." She bites her nail, a habit I haven't seen her perform in the time I've spent with her. Her description of Nick is spot on. He's the mastermind behind this whole thing, and inside his men are dying. I'll find out how many and who opposed me later on, but right now it's time for me to stop hiding and take back what is rightfully mine.

"Come on out, Dominic. You're not getting out of this alive. My men are inside slaughtering yours." Nick's cockiness infuriates me. I lift both hands in surrender as I slowly stand, knowing the nine-mil in my hand is nearly empty anyway. With one bullet left, I'll need the three-eighty strapped to my back.

"Stay down, no matter what you hear," I hiss at Nanette without even looking at her. As my head rises above the edge of the dumpster, I'm most in danger, but I have a feeling Nick won't just blow my head off. He's too cocky for that. He will rub it in first, talk himself up. So, I stand with boldness, gun pointed to the sky.

"Drop it," he says, his own weapon pointed at me.

I toss the gun to the pavement beside the dumpster and keep my hands in the air. Nick stares up at me then gestures with his gun. "Get out."

I follow his orders, leaping out of the dumpster with one solid push. I put all my weight on my right arm as my feet sail over the edge and land on the ground. My left shoulder hurts so badly I almost cry out, but I won't show him any weakness. This man is a disease, and he's going to die. It makes sense now, how he would be behind this. He hated my mother because Dad wouldn't make him the next in line for his throne. Mom made sure that I was the one to get that honor.

"You really hired the same motherfucking Italian to hunt me down? The same one..." I think of the scar across my chest and regretted having Jimmy pull that trigger. That man deserved a personal dose of justice, but not as much as the one in front of me.

"I did... Poetic right?" He scoffs and moves a step closer. I hear Nanette moving in the dumpster behind me, but I don't look. I can't take my eyes off this asshole for a single second.

"You're going down, Nick. You don't even see it yet." I stand with both hands raised, though not quite as high, and I take a step closer to him.

"I don't think you understand how this works, Dominic. I have too many men on my side. I tried to tell you my guys are inside slaughtering yours."

I listen to the keen of men dying, though the gunfire has now ceased. I'm surprised Leo hasn't reached out the window to pop Nick off, but it's possible he's taken a hit, or maybe his ammo ran out again.

"I'm not sure you know what's happening in there."

Nick's weapon lowers at my word and he chambers a round, pointing the barrel right at my chest. "You're as good as dead now. And even if I'm not the one to take that spot, your brother will do what we tell him. Men are on their way even now to kill Alexsi."

"My father? Leave him out of this," I snarl, ready to reach for my gun, but like this, out in the open, I'll be dead before it's drawn.

"Yeah, your father. How did you think we were going to pull this off?" He chuckles madly and for a second his eyes shut. I start to reach for my gun, knowing it's my one chance, when something soars over my shoulder. A fleeting shadow appears overhead, then whatever it is slams into his forehead. It gives me just the time I need to draw my gun and chamber a round. I point it at his leg and pull the trigger, hitting him just above the knee.

"Fuck!" Nick shouts, falling to the ground. His weapon clatters away from him and I rush over and kick it farther away.

"You were saying?" I hover over him, gun pointed at his head. We're only steps from my nine-mil, so I pick it up and aim my three-eighty at his other leg.

"God, Dominic, you can't be serious. You aren't getting out of this alive. You kill me, you won't survive a day."

Shot twice, once in each leg, and he still thinks he's victorious. He has no clue what my loyal men are capable of. I glance over my shoulder at Nanette who stands in the dumpster chest deep, staring at me.

"Turn away, Nan," I tell her, but she shakes her head.

This is going to scare her for life, but if she refuses to turn away, I can't help her. I drop the nine-mil on his chest, knowing there is but one bullet.

"You're insane. I could kill you now." Nick grabs the gun weakly and points it up at me.

"But you won't." Movement at the end of the alley catches my eye. It's my brothers, all four of them, walking toward me with arms in hand. "Because the moment you do, they will slaughter you." I nod at them, and Nick looks that direction and pales.

"Fuck, Dom, just shoot me. Put me out of my misery." His tune changes so fast I have to laugh at him.

"Your misery? You let that Italian trash rape my mother and destroy her so much that she killed herself. You're going to follow her now into that hell."

"What?" he asks, trembling. He tosses the gun, but I kick it back at him.

"Kill yourself, Nick. It's what you deserve, because it's what you did to her. And you should do it before they get here. Because if they know you're the one who set that whole thing up, they won't let you die. They'll torture you for months."

Nick is shaking, sweating so bad perspiration trickles down his face. He picks up the gun and points it at his head. "Dom, please."

"Fucking do it, Nick."

The bang resounds just as Sven reaches my side, and Nick's head lolls to the back, skull half gone. Blood and brain matter splatter across the front of his car, and I take a knee. I'm in so much pain I don't think I can breathe anymore.

It's over.

My mother's killer is avenged. The mole is rooted out. And I have Nanette.

Now, as long as she isn't so traumatized, she can't be around me, I'll have the life I want—finally.

22

NANETTE

I n my mind I picture the blood everywhere. Again—the same way it was when they nearly killed Jimmy. It torments me, even when Dominic walks me up to my room. He can barely breathe. He's in so much pain, but I can't function. The fear gnaws at my conscience. I've been here, this hell I'm living right now, and I fought to get out. How did I get back here? Why did I let this family suck me in?

"Jimmy," I whimper, but Dominic uses his right hand in the small of my back to guide me toward the bed. I'm covered in blood too, Dominic's blood. The minute the scarred man was dead, I was on him. He collapsed onto the ground, and I was there, putting pressure on the wound. His brothers said it was a through and through and taking him to the hospital was dangerous. I know he needs stitches, but he's trying to act brave, even with his jacket sleeve still tied around the seeping wound.

"Jimmy will be here later, Nan. Just get out of those bloody clothes and let me help you into bed."

I obey on autopilot. It's one thing I've learned to do now. First my clothing comes off, then my dignity is washed away as I stand nearly naked, still blood-stained, before him. Only his eyes aren't devilishly devouring me this time. He's hurting, and I'm hurting for him.

"Let me help you," I tell him, forcing him to sit on the edge of the bed. He listens and I go to the nightstand drawer where I saw a pair of scissors at one point. I pull them out and begin cutting his clothing away. He's wealthy enough to replace it all in a moment's notice but undressing him this way will eliminate some of his pain.

"Ouch," he winces as I get to the thick knot of his sleeve. It's tied tightly, but the scissors make short work of the fabric. He sits topless, a tiny trickle of blood running down his chest.

"You need a doctor. Antibiotics at the very least." I use a scrap of fabric to wipe away the blood, but he is stained just like me. He grabs my wrist and stops me, and I fear I've hurt him more, but he brings my hand to his lips and kisses it.

"I thought I lost you, and that thought drove me mad with rage. You are mine, Nanette. I wasn't joking when I said that." His eyes search me and after what we've been through today, I know I'm his. It's all I want to be.

"I know, Dom." I don't even pull my hand away from him. He kisses it again. For the first time in my life, it's not about power. It's not about dominating someone or using my ability or body to get them to do what I want. It's not about taking back what someone stole, or having my voice heard. When Dominic's eyes graze over my naked chest, I feel vulnerable, and I like it. I like that he looks at me like that, with hungry eyes. I like that I'm weak before him, that he is stronger than me, and more powerful.

"I'm going to need your help with my belt," he said quietly, and I look down, seeing the growing bulge in his pants. I reach down and undo his belt and the fly of his slacks, and he stands next to me. I slide his pants and boxers down over his hips, and he kicks off his shoes and steps out of his clothing. At the same time, I push my panties down and wait for him to be ready for me.

"Dom, you don't have to—"

"Nan…" He cuts me off. His tone is stern, but not angry. He stares into my eyes, but I don't see the same hungry animalistic passion there that I've seen before. He uses his right hand to stroke his cock, readying it for me, but I can't see how he's even going to do this. He can't use his left arm right now.

"Dominic…" I mutter, sighing. It's not that I don't want him. There is nothing more I want in this moment than to have him, but I don't want what I normally want. I don't even know how to express what I want.

He crawls onto the bed and carefully lays on his back, jerking his chin upward at me. Being on top, dominating him, it's the last thing I want. I fight it, shaking my head, but he uses one finger to call me closer, and like a trained pet I crawl toward him.

"I don't want…" I start to say, but I don't know how to say this.

"I know what you want." He nudges my leg and I straddle him, letting my slit rest against his hard cock.

"You do?"

"Yes, I do," he whispers.

"But I don't even know. I don't know what I want." I shake my head. I'm not sure what I'm trying to say. I'm lost in the moment. I'm lost in the look in his eyes. I'm lost in the feel of him, the smell of him, the taste of him. I'm lost, but I feel like I'm exactly where I'm supposed to be. I feel like this is where I'm supposed to be.

I kiss him, gently, and he kisses me back. I moan as I do, it's what I always want to do with him. He's the perfect man, and every time I kiss him, every time I touch him, I'm reminded of this fact. I slide my body over his cock, letting it rub against my slit, and he groans.

"I don't want to be in control."

He sits up and I wrap my arms around his neck, pressing my breasts against him. His hands slide down over my ass, feeling the curve there, and he squeezes it, spanking me gently. I yelp a little, and he laughs, then I laugh with him. "You want to ride me, Nan." His voice is a low, husky growl. He slides his hips forward and pushes the tip of his cock inside me.

I moan, "Oh," and nod my head. I do want to ride him.

As I sink down on his cock, using my knees to brace myself, my muscles tighten and my body quivers. I'm the one in control, but I feel like I have no control at all. He is in control of my body, of my actions, of my whole being. His eyes are fixed on mine, but I can't decipher the emotion inside of them. I stare at him until I feel like I'm going to lose my mind.

And then I know what I want—not to be in control, and not to dominate him. Not for him to dominate me either. I want us to be one. I want us to be one body, one heart, one soul. I want us to be together as one, and not in any way that means I'm not me and he's not him. I don't want us to lose ourselves. I don't want us to become one person. I just want us to be together. I want to be a part of him, and for him to be a part of me.

I stare into his eyes, into the dark green depths of his soul and I know I'm right. I know that this is what I want. I want to be with him, in every way. I want to be his. I want to belong to him, completely and forever. "I want to be joined with you," I whisper. "I want to feel you inside of me and feel your body against mine."

"Join with me, then," he whispers, slamming himself harder into me. He holds his arms out, wrapping them around me, pulling me close. "Come here." I can't move; his cock is deep inside of me, and I don't want to move away from it. He slams into me again, and my pussy tightens around him. He grunts and his fingers dig into my flesh. He's holding me so tight I'm not sure how I'll get away from him. If I ever want to get away from him.

The tears spill out of my eyes, and I don't even try to stop them. I don't feel ashamed or embarrassed, I just feel like they're right. I feel like they're justified. I want this. I need this. I need him. I need him to be my Dom. I need him to be in control, I need to submit to him. I need him to tell me what to do, and I need to do it. I need him to take my body and my heart and my soul. I need him to take them all, and I need to give them to him.

I ride him, slamming my body down on his as he holds me close to him, our bodies and souls becoming one. I feel as if I'm floating, and the moment I think about it, I realize I am. I'm floating, away from my body, away from this moment, and toward something I don't understand.

"Take me," I whisper, as I open my eyes and stare at him. "Take my body, my heart, my soul." He closes his eyes, and he grunts, spanking me hard, and I feel my body tighten around him. I'm on the edge of a climax, and I can feel my body tensing for it. I don't need to touch myself, or rub myself, or do anything else. All I need to do is feel him inside of me and it's enough to drive me over the edge.

He stares at me but doesn't say anything. He just lets me take him, and he lets me be in control. He doesn't struggle to get away from me or try to get back on top. He lets me have my way with him.

I ride him hard and fast, slamming my body down on his.

"Come," he says, and I do. I come, hard, and he does too. He comes with me, and he comes in me, filling me with his seed, uniting us, joining us together. I collapse on top of him, and he holds me close, stroking my hair, my face, my back. I can feel his cock inside of me, his arms wrapped around me. I feel his hands gently caressing me, possessively, as if he understands what I've given him just now.

And then I feel it, a feeling I've never felt, the total and complete sensation of being home. I don't know what it means. I don't know why I feel it, but I know that it's real. I know that it exists. And I know it's him. I know that it's what I've always wanted.

"You need to rest," he says, kissing the top of my head.

What I really need is for him to hold me, but sleep tugs at my eyelids. It's emotion-induced, but the day has worn on me. I want to see Jimmy, but maybe I'll just take a short nap. I roll off of him and before my head hits the pillow I sleep.

23

DOMINIC

Nanette is already snoring lightly by the time I finally get my pants on and buckled. My arm hurts like hell, but I have to learn to manage. She's right. I need my doctor to come give me a checkup and some antibiotics, but connecting with her was far more important to me than that.

I head down to my office with only minutes to spare. I told Jimmy two hours and in just a few minutes that threshold will pass. I've already made the plans; I was simply waiting on him to finish his first task. This next one will seem like a cake walk for him if he does it as I have planned for him. Everything fell into place the moment Gallagher walked into that restaurant. That, too, was planned. I'm sure both Jimmy and Nanette realize that now.

Nanette has changed too. The way she interacts with me, the way she fucks me, even her tone of voice. She's different—whole even. The most intriguing part of this whole thing to me is that she didn't need revenge on Gallagher to be whole. Just learning to trust that I keep my word was enough to bring her out of that cave of trauma-fueled fear. Jimmy, on the other hand, still needs justice.

I sit behind my desk, thirsty for a drink of my Scotch, but I know that will only thin my blood and I need the doctor to stitch me up before I go doing that. So, I abstain, though the drink would also help me deal with the excruciating pain.

Jimmy walks in on the hour, exactly when he is supposed to be here. I look up from my sleepy, pain-induced haze, and nod at the chair across from me. He stares at my shirtless body, blood still seeping slowly from the bullet hole in my shoulder. The blood smears down my chest and arms, dripping from my fingertips. Two inches lower and I'd have been breathing blood, but lucky for me Nick was a horrible shot.

Bruises and cuts litter my skin—some old, some new, almost like a topographical map. "So, you got him?" Jimmy says as he sits. He stares at the bullet hole as if it reminds him of the one given to him years ago. It isn't my first injury like this, and I'm sure it won't be my last. It may not be Jimmy's last either, the one Gallagher gave him. Not if he accepts my proposal which I'm about to offer him.

"Yeah, I got him." I nod slowly and my eyes feel heavy. "He's dead, along with at least ten others who united with him to overturn my authority." I lick my teeth, tasting Nanette's sweat on my lips as I do. Jimmy eyes me nervously.

"Am I done then? Are Nanette and I free to go?" He shifts in the chair, folding his hands together before pulling them apart and fiddling with the ring on his right hand. I can see he is scared of me; it's a good place to be. It's always a good place to be.

"Well, there is the matter of one of my family members dying that we need to discuss." I reach out with my right hand and open my top desk drawer. The forty-four magnum that I keep there is loaded, ready for use, and I pull it out and lay it on the desk facing Jimmy. He blanches, licking his lips and scooting back into the seat as if the gun is a rabid dog that may jump out and bite him.

"I didn't kill any of your family, Dominic. Just the Italian." His voice is full of tremors, shaking as much as his hands now do. He thinks I will kill him over this, which shows me how little he truly knows me. I could potentially cut him loose, swear him to secrecy, and let him live his life. I have enough dirt on him and proof of his involvement, that if he turns against me, I can turn him in just as easily. He'd go down along with the ship. But there is this small matter I promised Nanette.

"Red didn't deserve to die on the street in front of your house, James." I use his given name and he sobers, swallowing hard. His Adam's apple bobs, fear flooding his eyes.

"Look, Dom, I couldn't have known they were coming to get him." Jimmy holds his hands up defensively and shakes his head. "That wasn't my fault."

"If you had killed that Italian when you were supposed to, gotten me the information about the mole sooner, we wouldn't be having this conversation." I nudge the gun and nod at it. "Pick it up."

He swallows again, hesitating. His eyes dart to the weapon then back to my face. "Dom... I..."

"Don't piss me off, Jimmy. Pick up the fucking gun." I glare at him until he picks it up. "How does it feel?" I ask, probing him. He looks at me nervously. He thinks he can shrink back into the darkness of my office and vanish, but he doesn't know what I have planned for him.

"I don't know what you mean."

"I mean, how does it feel knowing you have justice within your reach?"

"Dom, I'd never do that. I won't kill you."

That's a lie. Given the right means, opportunity, and motive, anyone would kill me. I'm not a stupid man. Jimmy is as base as the rest of us. An Italian could walk up to him tomorrow and pay him ten million and I'm as good as dead. What I'm offering him is way more than that

—something that will prove his loyalty to me and Nanette and secure him a place in my family forever. He may not be blood, but after this, I'll consider him as much.

"Gallagher will be at the opera house on Hoewisher Street, Tuesday night at seven p.m. for an evening showing of Madam Butterfly. You will go in the back entrance using that gun." I talk calmly, and he looks down at the weapon. The silencer is built in, which will make it even easier for him. "He will be in box twelve, alone. His wife will suddenly be sick right before it is time to leave, and since he is due to meet a foreign dignitary immediately following, he will not be late."

"What?" Jimmy acts confused.

"I'm handing you revenge on a silver platter, Jimmy. There are no surveillance cameras in the theater, no guards, no security even. He won't be expecting it." I stare at him, and he shakes his head.

"What's the catch?" he asks, turning the weapon over and over in his hand.

"As I said, a member of my family is dead." I purse my lips and think about this one last time. I have no doubt in my mind that Jimmy is the only man for this job. "Red was my personal confidant. He got me intel when I needed it. He handled difficult tasks, had connections all over the city. He's gone. His spot needs to be filled."

"I... I don't understand." Jimmy's breathing is erratic, probably his pulse too. He is still shaking his head like a fool. I have to spell it out for him, or he won't get it.

"You are being given a chance at redemption. Nanette deserves her revenge, and so do you. I know what he did to you both. Gallagher, much like the Italian, has to pay. I've set everything up for you. You just have to walk in, pull the trigger, and walk out. That's it. If you want, you can even torture him a little. The boxes at the opera house are soundproof." I lower my chin, looking down my nose at him.

"But... why?" Jimmy's brows knit together in confusion still and he lets the gun rest on his lap.

"Because when I meet someone who is capable of the things of which I am also capable, I believe them worthy of working close to me. I'm the most powerful man in this city. You think it's the mayor or the commissioner—I have them on speed dial—because they need me, Jimmy. Now, all you have to do is finish what you started years ago. You finish Gallagher, prove to me and to your sister that you have what it takes, and you'll be my right-hand man."

Jimmy fumbles for a moment, reaching into his pocket. He pulls out a handkerchief that has a bit of blood stain on it and tosses it onto my desk. "Isn't that proof? The finger of the Italian, like you asked."

"Bring me Gallagher's and Nanette will know you have finished the job. Or would you like me to give her the gun?"

He squirms uncomfortably. I understand the dynamic between Jimmy and Nanette more clearly than ever. He feels ashamed that she has been the one to protect him all these years. It is that shame that has held him back, made him feel like less of a man. It's that shame that caused him to delay this job and fail me time and again. When Gallagher is dead, Nanette will be able to rest, and Jimmy will feel like the most powerful man in the world.

"So, are you going to do it?" I ask, waiting for his reply.

"Tuesday at seven, the opera house on Hoewisher?"

"Don't be late."

Jimmy stands, tucking the gun into his waistband, and walks to the door.

"Make no mistake, Jimmy," I call to him. He stops and looks back at me. "Your sister is mine now. If you fuck up, you die. I can't stop Gallagher's people from coming for you. But if you succeed, you have the entire Bratva at your back. You'll never want for anything again, and Nanette won't either."

Jimmy walks out without saying another word, and for a few moments I am alone. I sit with my thoughts for a while, wondering if he will have the guts to do it. If not, I will finish Gallagher myself, just to spare Nanette the gory action. She is too precious to see that event again. After watching Nick die today, that's all the bloodshed I ever want to see her witness again.

I shoot my doctor a text message letting him know I need him to come over, then I lean back in my chair. It's been a hell of a day, and it's not over. I assume the stitches will hurt like hell too; doc isn't always gentle, but I have walked away from this with my life. The mole is rooted out, and my family is safe. I think about calling my father, but it can wait until morning. Sven too; he will want to know how I plan to reorganize things now that so many of our people have revealed how compromised they are.

"Dom?"

I look up to see Nanette standing in the doorway. She is wearing one of my white t-shirts and a pair of pink panties. She's gorgeous, even with the blood still caked to her hands. Later, I will soak her in a hot bath and wash her, clean myself, but now I gesture to her.

"Come, sit with me," I tell her, and she climbs right onto my lap. Her body curls up on my chest, fragile and emotional.

"You said Jimmy was coming?" she asks, resting her forehead against my neck. The scent of our sex still lingers on her skin. I like it that way. I'm like a dog who has marked his territory. I want to make her smell like me in every way so every man will know she is mine forever.

"He just left." I kiss her hair and hold her as tightly as I can with my right arm. She plays with my chest hair, picking the blood out of it.

"I hoped to see him."

"He'll be back. He's fine. Now my men are watching him, and he will be safe. No one is going to harm him, Nan."

She feels good in my arms, a goodness I never thought was my right to enjoy. Since the day my mother died, I felt like I only deserved tragedy, pain, sadness. But this victory, no matter how small it may seem on the outside, has taught me that I can't blame myself for other people's evil. Watching the closeness between Jimmy and Nanette showed me that family is everything, though I think I knew that already.

Nan sucks in a deep breath like she's going to say something, but she says nothing. I can tell she is antsy, though I don't know if she wants to ask me something or if it is because when she climbed on my lap my wound started bleeding again. She touches the sticky flow lightly and then presses her index finger to her thumb and rubs the blood around.

"And Gallagher?" she says, her voice just a whisper.

With confidence, I reply, "Jimmy is handling that, and when he's done, he will prove to you that you never have to fear anything again."

Nan looks up at me with fear in her eyes. "But last time—"

"Isn't going to happen again. Your brother is ready this time."

She stares at me for a moment and then lays her head back down. She is so different now, not questioning me anymore, not angry at all. To think a week ago she couldn't stop herself from screaming at me, and now she curls up on my chest feeling safe.

I reach into my desk drawer again; this time it's not a gun I'm after. I rifle around a bit amongst the paper clips and thumbtacks, and I find what I'm looking for. I slip the tip of my finger into the ring and pull it out, shutting the drawer again. As I hold it in front of Nanette's face, she gasps and covers her mouth.

"I've seen that…"

"Yes, because you went through my things." I brandish the diamond and pearl ring that was featured on my mother's hand in the photos in the old picture album. "It is my mother's ring. I took it from her finger as I lay bleeding out next to her. Put it on." I hand the ring to Nanette, and she hesitates.

"Dominic, I—"

"Put it on," I order, and she sits up, offering a look of shame. She slides the ring onto her finger slowly but doesn't make eye contact with me. "You're going to be my wife now."

"Is that a proposal?" she asks, turning her chin up so that our eyes meet.

"It's an order."

A smile curls the corner of her lip, and she leans down to kiss me, but the moment our lips brush against one another, I wince in pain. She braces herself on my chest and the blood flows more quickly out of the wound.

"Fuck, I'm sorry," she says leaping up, and I chuckle, coughing a few times.

"It's okay. The doctor is on the way to do some stitches."

She grins at me and grabs some tissues to cover the wound. "It's about time you do what I tell you," she jokes playfully. I can't wait to make this woman my wife. It's the only thing left on my list.

24

NANETTE

This garden has quickly become my favorite place on Dominic's property. I sit at a small wrought iron patio table, painted white to match the trellis under which it sits. The garden is a beautiful oasis filled with blooming flowers of every color imaginable. The air is thick with the sweet scent of jasmine and lavender. A small fountain burbles in the corner, its gentle melody providing a backdrop to the chirping of birds and buzzing of bees. The sunlight filters through the leaves of the trees, creating dappled patterns on the ground below. It is a peaceful retreat, a place to escape the chaos of the world outside.

The past week has been a complete hurricane of emotion and problems. I've barely had a chance to catch my breath, let alone process everything that's happened. My mind keeps going back to that warehouse, replaying the events over and over again like a broken record. But as I sit here in this tranquil garden, I finally feel like I can start to let go of some of that trauma. My mind can rest, even if it's just for a little while.

But my tranquility is shattered when I hear the sound of footsteps crunching on the gravel path. Lost in my thoughts, I didn't notice the figure approaching until he's standing right in front of me. I look up to see Jimmy, a small smile playing on his lips. Dominic stands behind him, stoic as usual. Jimmy welcomes me with open arms when I pop out of my seat to run to him. I feel like it's been months; in reality it's been only days.

"Oh my god, I thought I'd never see you again," he says, wrapping me in the tightest bear hug I've felt in years. He squeezes me so hard I can barely breathe, and I pat him on the back to break free.

I take a step back and look at him, noticing the bruises on his cheek and the cuts on his knuckles. My heart sinks. "What happened to you?" I ask, my voice shaky. While I'm grateful he's alive, I'm upset he's been hurt. My only thought is about his well-being. That's the way it's always been, ever since that night with Gallagher.

Jimmy shrugs. "Just a little scuffle. No big deal." He brushes off my concern, but it doesn't help me relax.

Dominic clears his throat, drawing our attention. "I'll leave you two to catch up. I have some business to attend to," he says before walking away.

Jimmy takes a seat across from me and I notice that he's fidgeting with his hands. "I'm sorry, sis," he says, his voice low. "I didn't mean to drag you into all of this."

I shake my head. "Don't be ridiculous, Jimmy. I'm just glad you're safe and sound." I sit on the edge of my seat, ready to hear the gory details. I know how bad things went on my end; how dangerous it was. Jimmy can't even look me in the eye right now, shame over getting me tangled up in his ordeal. It's over. That's all I care about.

He nods, but I can see that he's still holding something back. "There's something else," he says, hesitating. I notice a different look in his eye, one that puts me more at ease the minute his gaze meets mine.

"What is it?" I lean forward, watching his expression carefully.

Jimmy takes a deep breath before speaking. "It's Gallagher," he says, voice steady and even. I've never heard him say the man's name with such a calm tone. He doesn't even break eye contact.

I nod slowly, my heart racing. That night is still fresh in my mind, and the thought of that man sends shivers down my spine. After the encounter at that restaurant, he's been in my dreams, in my waking hours; he haunts me and makes me feel paranoid. Dominic promised to help me get my revenge. Is this how?

"I found him," Jimmy continues, his voice low and dangerous. "And I took care of him."

My eyes widen as I realize what he means. "You...you mean you...?" I feel my breath catch in my throat.

Jimmy nods, his expression unapologetic. "I killed him, sis. I made him pay for what he did to you—to us."

I can hardly believe what I'm hearing. It's like a weight has been lifted off my shoulders that I've carried for more than a decade. I've been avenged, and Jimmy is the one who did it. Not by my hand as I would have liked, but he's gone, and Jimmy got his revenge too. I notice a new strength in his eyes now, something he may never have had if he hadn't done this on his own.

Gallagher nearly killed Jimmy, after forcing him to watch that. I know how much that affected Jimmy for years. He spent all these years as a trained killer, trying to find a way to give me the justice I deserved—we deserved—the exact same way I have lived every single day trying to get my voice back, my power. Dominic knew what he was doing. The entire time, this is what he had planned. My eyes well up.

For a moment, the garden is quiet, only the chirping birds around me. I'm not sure what to say, how to react. Part of me is grateful to Jimmy, for taking revenge on my behalf. But another part of me is scared, wondering if this will all come back to haunt us, if someone will know it was him.

Finally, I find my voice. "Thank you," I say, my voice barely above a whisper. "Thank you for doing that for me."

Jimmy smiles, his eyes softening. "Since the moment that bastard touched you it's all I've thought about. I will sleep easier tonight."

I nod, feeling a sense of relief wash over me. For the first time in years, I feel safe. And it's all thanks to Jimmy and Dominic. I never for a second thought I'd feel this way about Dominic, but I do, and I like that I do. Being the strong one all the time has exhausted me. I'm grateful to have two men to protect me now, ones I trust with my life.

I reach out and take Jimmy's hand, but he pulls away and reaches into his pocket. When his hand emerges again, he has a ring in it. It's a thick gold band with any onyx stone set to the backdrop of small diamonds. I've seen that ring far too many times, felt the sting of it as it came down over my cheek too. It's Gallagher's ring. I blink and tears rush down my cheeks. He really has done it.

"I brought this for you, as proof that he really is gone. You can rest now, Nan." He places the ring in my palm, and I clasp my hand around it, weeping for a moment. The nightmare of my past is now over. Healing can come, for both me and Jimmy. I can only cover my mouth and cry.

Moments later, Dominic emerges from the path, carrying a tray of drinks and a bottle of Scotch. I look up as he sets the tray on the table and when I rise, he hugs me. He's tender now, brushing my hair away from my face and kissing my forehead. It's as if he has changed too; as if avenging his mother has given him the peace he needs to be here for me.

"It's over," I whisper, and he nods, his lips still pressed against my forehead.

"We have a new agreement though," Jimmy says, interrupting.

I wipe my eyes and sit back down, and Dominic joins us, sitting close to me.

Jimmy clears his throat and speaks up. "I'm staying on with Dominic, Nan. We both agreed that we can do better together than apart. It's going to be dangerous and risky, but it's what's right. We want to make sure no one else has to go through what you did."

I nod, knowing that Jimmy and Dominic are a force to be reckoned with.

"So, you're just going to be a hitman for the Bratva?" I glance at Dominic, nervous for what this means for Jimmy.

Jimmy looks at me with a soft smile. "It's more than that, Nan." There is a twinkle of pride in his eyes, and I can't help but feel happy for him, even though I know teaming up with Dominic is dangerous business. I look down at the ring in my palm, then at the ring on my finger.

"I have something to say too," I tell him, reaching out for Dominic. He takes my hand and squeezes it. "I'm going to marry Dom." Jimmy's eyes widen in surprise, and he looks at Dominic, then back at me. "Are you sure, Nan?" he asks cautiously.

I nod, feeling a sense of determination wash over me. "Yes, I am sure," I reply firmly. "Dominic has been there for me through everything, and I know he will always be there for me. I love him, Jimmy. I want to spend the rest of my life with him."

Dominic's hand tightens around mine. I know he will never admit to loving me; maybe it shows him as being weak. But I know he loves me in his own way. I may just be an object in the way he talks about me to other people, but no one has ever known me the way he does, not even Jimmy.

Jimmy looks between us for a moment, then lets out a deep sigh. "Alright," he says at last. "If that's what you both want, I won't stand in your way." He doesn't look the happiest, but we are all in this together now.

"It's what I want," I tell him and I'm certain it is.

I see Dominic rise and walk to the fountain, his head low, and eyes looking to the ground as he walks. I sip my Scotch and set the glass down before I rise and follow him to the fountain, which is roaring with water, the spray of the white foam misting the air, creating a cool rainfall all around us. The sound of water bubbling from the fountain is a calming melody against the background of all that has happened in the past week. As I approach, I see the brick with the inscription of a woman's name. I know in my heart this is a memory stone, laid here after his mother was laid to rest.

Though Dominic rises, he remains hunched over, head lowered to the ground. His gaze is towards the ground, and I can only guess at what emotions are stirring within him. His hair hangs down in strands, his eyes are rimmed in darkness and his lips are turned down. I reach out and touch Dominic's hand, which is gripping the fountain. His hand feels rough and calloused. I run my hand across it and look up at him, his hand still gripping the fountain, his breathing heavy, eyes focused on the ground in front of him.

"Are you okay?" I ask cautiously, and he nods.

"You're right. It's over." His gruff voice is filled with grief, and I understand completely.

I step closer to him, my body touching his, as I tilt my head up to look at him. I place my hand over his heart, feeling the rapid thumping beneath my palm. He flinches at my touch, but he doesn't pull away. Instead, he leans into me, his forehead resting against mine.

"I know it hurts," I whisper, my breath mingling with his. "But we have each other."

He nods, his grip on the fountain loosening as he wraps his arms around me, pulling me closer to him. I can feel the heat of his body against mine, and I know my words have brought some comfort to him. I close my eyes, allowing myself to get lost in the moment, in the feel of his arms around me, in the scent of his cologne.

When I pull away, I know the only way for me to let go and move on, is to remove any trace I have of Gallagher. I look down at the ring then glance at Jimmy. He nods, understanding my unspoken words, and we both know what needs to be done. I take a deep breath before getting down on my knees. The stone is hard beneath my knees, and I can feel the coldness seeping through my jeans. But I ignore the discomfort, focusing on the task at hand. With trembling fingers, I dig into the earth, feeling the dirt and soil give way to my touch. It takes a few minutes, but finally, I hit something hard, and I know I've reached the spot where I need to bury the ring.

It's a token of my freedom, but it's also a symbol of a past that I need to leave behind. I close my eyes, taking a deep breath, and then I drop the ring into the hole. I cover it with dirt, patting it down gently, before standing up. Jimmy is standing a few feet away, watching me with a somber expression.

"It's done," I say softly, my voice barely above a whisper. "I'm ready to move on now." He nods, understanding, and then he takes my hand. We walk away from the stone, leaving the ring buried beneath it. It feels like a weight has been lifted off my shoulders, and I know that I can finally start a new chapter in my life.

We walk back and join Jimmy at the table. As we sit there, sipping on Scotch and talking about our plans for the future, I can't help but feel grateful for the two men sitting beside me. They've given me a sense of safety and security that I never thought was possible. And as we clink our glasses together, I know that together, we can take on anything that comes our way.

The sun begins to set, casting a warm glow over us, and I lean back in my chair, feeling content. It's been a long journey, but I've finally found my place in this world, thanks to Jimmy and Dominic. And as I look out at the view, with the two men I love by my side, I know that I'm exactly where I'm meant to be.

A few months ago, I never imagined that I would be free from that trauma. I believed no counselor in the world could untie the knots in my heart. Since Dominic barged into my life, it feels like everything is upside down—but in a good way. I feel lighter, happier, more at ease. I can breathe now, and dream again. And that is more than anyone could ever ask for.

25

DOMINIC

I sit in my office waiting. This damn tuxedo is uncomfortable as hell, but it's my wedding day. But even on my wedding day, the job doesn't stop. Father is getting sicker now, and I'm being asked to take over more responsibility, which means I need to clean up any loose ends after everything that happened last month. After the shooting that happened on the dock, we had a lot of unwanted attention with the police, and I let Sven handle everything. Now I need to know he's done the job right.

He walks into my office with confidence, parking himself across from my desk.

"I assume everything has been taken care of?" I ask, confident that he's done his job well.

Sven nods. "Yeah, Dom. The cops are off our backs and the mole is dead. We made sure his body will never be found."

I nod, relieved. "Good. I can't have any loose ends on my wedding day."

Sven leans forward, studying my face. "How are you feeling, Dom? About everything that's happened?"

I can't help but let out a deep sigh. "Honestly, I don't even know. It's been such a whirlwind. I'm just trying to take it one day at a time." Knowing my mother can finally rest in peace because her attacker has been dealt a hand of justice is what I've wanted for decades now. Sven knows this; he's wanted it as much as me.

He nods in understanding, but there's a glint in his eye that suggests he's not done talking. "And what about Nanette? How are you feeling about her?"

I feel a warmth spread through me at the mention of her name. Nanette is like a freight train I never saw coming. I just wanted the man who hurt my mother to die, and along the way I met my match. I act aloof in front of Sven, but inside there is nothing that will ever make me happier than to marry Nanette and put babies in her belly.

"It will work out well." Men in my family don't get sappy over their women, and I'm almost the leader now. Sven understands this, and he offers a hand clap as he stands to his feet. I'm not finished with him though, so I call his name. "Sven."

He stops, shoving his hand into his pockets and stopping to hear what I have to say. "Yeah, Dom."

"You and Allie, what's going on there? I mean, your temper has been out of control. I heard from Leo how you handled things in that warehouse shootout. Some restraint may have kept the rollers off our back." I purse my lips, scowling at him. Sven gets out of control when things don't go the way he plans, and this thing with his would-be love has gotten him a hefty dose of unwanted attention lately.

"You know, Dom. Women..." He shrugs it off, but I am not pleased with his response. This woman isn't bad news for him; he could use a woman like her to remind him to keep his guard up and his head down, but he's being reckless when it comes to her ex-boyfriend, and people will start to notice if I don't force him to temper himself.

"Sven, you can't go off half-cocked. You're going to make people start watching you and if the wrong people are watching there will be nothing I or our father can do about it. You understand that?" I stand, straightening my tie as I do. It's almost time to walk down the aisle, and I just want this reprimand to be over now. I'm sure Sven does too.

"Look, Dom, I'm handling things. Now that the mole is done, I'm sure things with Allie will settle down. Okay?" He gives me a less-than-reassuring look and shakes his head before walking out.

I take a deep breath and try to shake off the tension that Sven's reck-lessness has brought upon me. I can't have any distractions today. I make my way toward the garden where the ceremony is about to take place. The sun is shining bright, casting a warm glow on everything around me. The garden is decorated beautifully, with soft pink and white flowers lining the aisle. The guests are already seated, waiting for my arrival.

The scent of the flowers is intoxicating, filling the air with their aroma. It's almost a little too much. It makes me think of summer, of youth and innocence. I'm far from innocent now, but Nanette deserves this after everything she's been through.

I stand at the edge of the aisle and watch as the bridesmaids make their way down, their pastel dresses flowing gracefully behind them. They're all beautiful, but none of them compare to Nanette. She's the epitome of elegance in her white, satin gown, and her hair is styled in soft curls that frame her face perfectly. As she makes her way toward me, I can't help but feel a sense of pride. She's mine now, and I'll do anything to protect her.

The priest begins the ceremony, and I listen intently to his words. I'm not a religious man, but there's something comforting about the ritual and tradition of a wedding. It makes me feel like everything is right in the world, even if it's only for a moment.

When it's time for the vows, Nanette turns to me, her eyes shining with unshed tears. "Dominic," she begins, her voice barely above a whisper. "I never thought I would find someone who could understand me the way you do. You've shown me what it means to love and be loved, and I promise to spend the rest of my life showing you the same."

I take her hands in mine, feeling a sense of warmth spread through me at her touch. "Nanette," I say, my voice low and steady. "I never thought I could find someone who would make me want to be a better man. You've shown me what it means to be selfless and to care for someone more than anything else in the world. I promise to protect you, to cherish you until the end of time."

As I speak, I feel a weight lifted off my shoulders. Nanette's presence has given me a sense of purpose that I never thought was possible. I've spent my life doing things that I'm not proud of, but with her by my side and my mother's attacker gone, I feel like I can finally start to make things right.

The priest nods at us, signaling that it's time to exchange rings. I slip the diamond band onto Nanette's finger, and she does the same for me. It's a small gesture, but it feels like we're making a promise to each other that's unbreakable.

The rest of the ceremony passes in a blur of happiness and joy. We kiss, and the guests cheer as we make our way back down the aisle. I can't believe I'm lucky enough to have found someone like Nanette. She's everything I never knew I needed, and I'll do anything to make sure she's happy.

The minute I kiss my bride, we are whisked away inside the house where Mika has planned our meal and baked a cake. Jimmy hovers near us, following my every step. It took some convincing to make my brothers accept him, but all is well in my world now. Besides, if marrying Nanette meant confirming him into the family, then I made the right choice. Now, if he can help keep Sven in line with this situation with Allie, we'll be doing okay.

If…

EXCERPT: SHE'S MINE

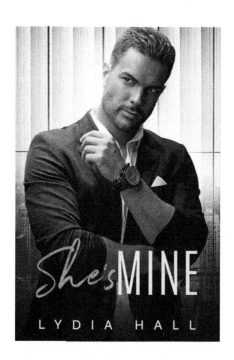

She needed protection when I was hired to guard her life.

And now... *I need to save her from myself.*

Alyssa is 15 years younger than me.

That's a problem but I want her every second of every day.

She feels safe when I put my arms around her.

Partying became her escape after the Bloodline Cartel murdered her brother.

And watching her become vulnerable with me has made me want her even more.

I'd turn the world upside down to keep her safe.

I told myself I'd keep my distance.

But I couldn't help pressing my lips against hers.

Life began feeling unreal with her before the darkness returned.

My ability to protect her would be tested when a secret comes out.

Along with *another* secret that's growing inside her.

I'd be damned if I let the enemies destroy my family.

She's mine – and always will be.

David

Returning to work after a break was always a little weird. I loved my job, I really did, but after two weeks in secluded luxury at my holiday home hidden away in the forest by Lake Arrowhead, I wasn't looking forward to returning to the hustle and bustle of central LA.

And I was even more surprised when I was going through my usual morning routine, and my phone started to ring.

The caller I.D on the screen told me it was my boss, Jeffrey Garcia was calling, which was odd considering I was due in the office in a couple of hours anyway.

I answered the phone, as I balanced my electric toothbrush in my mouth, and turned on the coffee maker.

"Hey, Jeffrey, what's up?"

"Ah, good, you're awake. David, I need you to come to the office as soon as possible."

Even though I couldn't see Jeffrey, I could hear the tension in his voice -- never a good sign.

I'd worked with Jeffrey and his company J&J Security for almost fifteen-years and knew Jeffrey to be a no-nonsense man who got straight to the point.

If he wanted me to come to the office A.S.A.P on my first day back after a vacation, instead of easing me back in with a simple case, I knew whatever he had to tell me was a big deal.

I switched off the coffee maker, knowing I could grab takeout on the way to the office, spat toothpaste into the sink and then said, "I'll be there in ten minutes."

I ended the call without another word, finished getting ready and then was in my Range Rover and driving across the city in record time. I stopped only briefly to grab a 'to-go' coffee, before pulling into my designated parking space in the J&J Security parking lot.

I entered the modern building that was situated in the central business district of downtown Los Angeles, and quickly greeted the receptionist Deborah on my way to the elevator.

"Welcome back, David. I hope you had a nice vacation."

"I did, thank you, Deborah," I said, giving the receptionist a dazzling smile. The woman put up with a lot working for J&J Security and was the first administrative employee anyone contacting the company would come into touch with. It was through her that all business flowed, and I knew much of J&J Security's administrative side would fall apart without Deborah and her team of assistants. "I'd love to stop and tell you all about it, but Jeffrey wants to see me in his office straight away."

Deborah gave me a knowing smile, and I had no doubt she already knew what was going on -- it had probably gone through her first.

"Yeah, good luck with everything. You're in for a wild first day back in the office."

As I strode to the elevator, I didn't doubt Deborah's words. I'd been working for J&J Security for the entirety of my adult life.

Growing up, it had just been me and my mom, and I'd fallen in with a bad crowd. I'd almost ended up in prison, but Jeffrey had saved me from that when he offered me a place in his company.

Since then, I'd worked my way up the ranks of J&J Security and was now one of Jeffrey's three most senior bodyguards. I'd seen a hell of a lot in my line of work, including brutal murders and gang-related coverups.

I knew whatever Jeffrey wanted to speak to me about would be serious.

I felt my heart hitch as I walked from the elevator to Jeffrey's office, slightly nervous about what I was about to be told. I took my job *very* seriously, and in the last few years, I'd watched the peace we'd forged with the LAPD slowly deteriorate as gang activity became more common. I had no doubt that whatever Jeffrey wanted to speak to me about, it involved LA's biggest threat -- the Bloodline Cartel.

I knocked on Jeffrey's office door, and a moment later, he called, "Come in."

As I entered the office, I was shocked by two things. First, it looked as though Jeffrey had aged at least ten years in the two weeks I'd been away on vacation. He had dark circles under his eyes, his skin was sallow, and his once lustrous black hair now had more gray streaked in it than ever.

The second sight that shocked me was the presence of Charles Blythe -- Police Commissioner of the LAPD.

Yeah, whatever was going on was very serious indeed.

"Thank you for getting here so quickly David," Jeffrey said in welcoming, gesturing to the empty seat next to Blythe and opposite himself. "You know Commissioner Blythe, of course."

I gave Blythe a polite smile and offered him my hand. "Good to see you again, Commissioner. I hope you're well."

Blythe grimaced as I took my seat. "I've been better."

"I'm sorry to hear that, Commissioner."

Charles Blythe was the same age as Jeffrey, and they were both twenty-five years my senior. From what Jeffrey had told me, he and Blythe had attended college together, and were good friends. Since they'd graduated, Blythe had worked closely with J&J Security, the police commissioner and my boss often collaborating on criminal cases. I only knew him in a professional sense, but Charles Blythe was a man not to be messed with. It was thanks to him that the LAPD had made any headway against the Bloodline Cartel at all.

Jeffrey steepled his fingers in front of him, and then took control of the conversation. "Charles is here today because he's in need of our services. Yours specifically, David."

I glanced from my boss to Blythe, surprised to learn the police commissioner had a need for me.

"The Bloodline are becoming more daring with their behaviour. In the last two weeks alone, three attempts have been made on my life.

I'm hiring J&J Security to serve as the personal security for myself and my family."

I gulped around a lump in my throat. After Jean Grant, the Mayor of LA, Charles Blythe was the most important person in the city.

"I've already spoken to Scott Payne," Jeffrey said, referencing one of the three senior members of J&J Security, along with myself and another experienced bodyguard, Pedro Lincoln. "And I'll be seeing Pedro straight after. I want all three of you on Commissioner Blythe's security detail. One team for Charles himself, a team for his wife Pamela, and another for their daughter, Alyssa."

Blythe had a daughter. I had no idea. I knew he had a son that had been caught up in the fight against the Bloodline many years ago, and sadly lost his life to the cartel. I'd never heard mention of a daughter though. Blythe must have kept her identity under wraps, which made sense, after losing his son.

From the corner of my eye, I caught Blythe wince at the mention of his daughter. "Alyssa can be a little *spirited*, shall we say."

"That's where you come in," Jeffrey continued. "While I have the uttermost faith in you, Payne and Lincoln, I feel you're most suited to dealing with delicate situations. I want you to serve as Alyssa's personal bodyguard."

I let out a long breath. Guarding the police commissioner of the LAPD was one thing. Guarding his only living child was a whole other matter.

I'd be safer handing myself over to the Bloodline than I would be facing Blythe if I let anything bad happen to his baby girl.

But I wasn't about to show any sign of weakness. I'd dealt with difficult clients, delicate situations and *spirited* charges plenty of times before, and had always managed to handle my business in the most professional manner.

I was sure Alyssa Blythe would be no different.

"I'll do my very best, Sir," I said, offering my assurances to both Jeffrey and Blythe. "What do I need to know about your daughter?"

Blythe smiled fondly. "As I said, she's a little spirited. Entirely mine and Pamela's fault. After we lost Joey, Alyssa was all we had, and well … we might have spoiled her a little. Here, see for yourself--"

Blythe pulled his phone out of his jacket pocket, tapped the screen a few times, and then handed the device to me.

The phone was open on the social media profile of the most stunning woman I'd ever seen. With a curvaceous figure, long black hair and bright blue eyes, it was clear Alyssa Blythe held the attention of every room she entered.

Alyssa's pictures showed her at various events, always surrounded by a crowd of people. She wore designer clothes and expensive jewellery, and her smile was bright and infectious.

As I stared at the images of Alyssa, I couldn't help but feel a sense of unease. It wasn't that I'd never seen a beautiful woman before -- I lived in LA. I was surrounded by gorgeous women all the time. But I'd never protected someone like Alyssa before, and I wasn't sure if I was up to the task.

Honestly, I couldn't help but feel a little intimidated.

I also couldn't help but assume that she was a princessy brat. Her father had already said as such, only in a much kinder way. Spirited was an easy code for a wild *child,* and I was worried that she would be difficult to control and that she wouldn't take the threat against her family seriously.

But as I continued to stare at Alyssa's pictures, I couldn't deny that there was something about her that intrigued me. I couldn't quite put my finger on it, but there was something different about Alyssa that

I'd never seen before in the socialites and ladies of high society you found in a city like LA.

"Obviously, I don't want anything to happen to myself or Pamela, either, but well..." Blythe shook his head. "You don't have children, do you, David?"

"Not yet, Sir. I've always been too focused on my career."

"Well, when you do become a father, you'll understand. Nothing compares to the pain of losing a child. When we lost Joey, it damn near tore me and Pamela apart. The only thing that even kept us going was Alyssa. I'd sooner die than let anything bad happen to her. Am I making myself clear?"

"Perfectly, Sir," I replied, knowing that if it was reported that even one hair on Alyssa's head was out of place, it would be *me* on the chopping block and no one else.

Usually, a case like this wouldn't have been an issue. I'd protected my fair share of high-profile clients. It was why I was amongst the top of Jeffrey's most trusted bodyguards.

What I'd never dealt with before was a young, rich, beautiful woman who was likely used to getting things her own way, never being told no, and having *everything* on her own terms.

I couldn't blame Charles and Pamela Blythe for spoiling their daughter, especially not after they'd lost their son. But knowing that didn't make my upcoming job any easier.

I had no doubt that Alyssa had her father wrapped around her little finger, and probably thought she could do the same to any man that came into her life.

Well, if Alyssa Blythe thought she was going to wrap *me* around her little finger, she had another thing coming. Like I'd said, I lived in LA. I was surrounded by gorgeous women all the time. Hell, I'd even dated a fair few. And none of them had *ever* stomped their feet and gotten their own way with me. Not even in my most serious relationship when I'd dated an up-and-coming actress, who now had a few Academy Awards to her name.

I wasn't about to let Alyssa Blythe be the first.

Read the complete story here!

SUBSCRIBE TO MY EXCLUSIVE NEWSLETTER

I hope you enjoyed reading this book.

If you want to stay updated on my upcoming releases, price promotions, and any ARC opportunities, then I would love to have you on my mailing list.

Subscribe yourself to my exclusive mailing list using the below link!

Subscribe to Lydia Hall's Exclusive Newsletter

Printed in Great Britain
by Amazon

36449391R00121